END OF THE INNOCENCE

by

Tracy McDonald

DORRANCE
PUBLISHING CO
EST. 1920
PITTSBURGH, PENNSYLVANIA 15238

Dorrance Publishing Co
585 Alpha Drive
Suite 103
Pittsburgh, PA 15238
Visit our website at *www.dorrancebookstore.com*

ISBN: 978-1-6442-6204-7
eISBN: 978-1-6442-6340-2

*This book is dedicated to Meagan Madden
who has taught me that no matter what life deals you
that we all have the strength to be survivors.*

CHAPTER ONE

The year was 2025, and in the immortal words of Ernest Hemingway, some might say the world is a fine place worth fighting for, but Paul Simon did not agree. He was a simple man with a quiet manner and a kind heart. He lived in the small town of Cold Spring in New York State. This town was known for its laid-back manner, and the people had a sort of infectious kindness. Although the population was only around two thousand, it was enough to keep Paul relatively busy most days with his medical practice. His wife of twenty years was a fiery redhead with very attractive features. Paul and Laura had relocated to Cold Spring approximately five years ago. After the death of their only daughter, they decided that a major change and a shift of their priorities was their only option. They simply had no desire to live in Manhattan any longer. While Manhattan was the smaller of the five boroughs of NYC, it still was an overpopulated, smelly hell hole in Paul's eyes. It had long ago lost its appeal to him. He endeavored to endure his life in the city because of his wife's desire. Up until Annie's death, Laura had viewed the city as cultured diverse place with endless exciting things to do and countless places to go. He swore she loved the fast-paced lifestyle, and he respected and adored her enough to stay.

He remembered the day it all changed like yesterday. Paul had spent an exhausting day at the office and had taken his usual ride home on the subway. Twenty minutes later, the two boys had arrived home and immediately took up the task of filling their faces with some unhealthy snack they had found in the cupboard. Laura would have taken it away and replaced it with an orange or apple, but Paul was not as strict and too tired to care. He stood with his elbow resting on the granite island, observing the boys with mixed amusement and childlike curiosity. They were engaged in some feud over a trivial incident that had occurred in the schoolyard earlier that day. This was normal behavior for the boys; they were always fighting over something. Jack and Paul junior where only two years apart, and Paul figured that the sibling rivalry was normal for two boys of eight and ten. Now Annie was the oldest, and although she was mature for a twelve-year-old, she still could be quite the drama queen at times. Laura was not home yet, but this was not unusual as she loved to shop after work. Annie was late, but Paul was not worried until the phone began to ring. As he picked it up, it still did not register that it even concerned his daughter; he totally expected it to be his wife or a neighbor or even a telemarketer. The moment the voice on the other end stated they were an officer from the NYPD named Officer Cleary, Paul knew it was not going to be good news. Nothing on earth could have ever prepared him for what the officer said next. "Sir, is this Paul Simon?" Even though he felt half sick and was not even sure why, he replied, "Yes," and the man went on to explain something had happened to his daughter, Annie. He did not want to elaborate over the phone, so he verified the address and explained he would be over in approximately a half hour and that it might be wise if his wife was present, then he hung up. Paul stood motionless for what seemed an eternity and did not snap out of it till he noticed both boys quietly staring at him. Deep in his soul he wanted to shield them, but he knew it was written all over his face. His hands were shaking, and little beads of sweat had formed on his forehead. He struggled hard to focus and maintain some kind of composure as he dialed the phone to contact his wife and the boy's uncle John.

Paul did not want to create panic, so he kept both calls short. After he finished, he turned his attention to his sons and instructed them both to go pack enough clothes for a two-day visit with their uncle. The boys looked at him with a puzzled look but did as they were told. Paul rarely drank, but he found himself pouring a stiff bourbon, and he belted it back and made one more with ice in it. He was pacing the apartment when his brother showed up. John was asking questions, and

Paul told him he would call with details later and collected the boys and their things and sternly told them all to please leave now. Ten minutes after they left, his wife showed up, and five minutes later, the officer arrived, too. The three of them exchanged polite greetings, and Paul placed the bottle of bourbon on the kitchen island with some ice and three glasses. His wife shot him an odd glance but said nothing. As they all sat down, and Officer Cleary began to speak. What followed was a gruesome tale of how the police had found their daughter's half-nude, mutilated body in Central Park around 2:00 P.M. that very afternoon. Paul sat motionless as he felt an eerie numbness sinking into his whole being. His wife was attempting to scream but all that was coming out her mouth were strange hisses and grunts. She abruptly stood up and fell to the floor and began crawling along with incoherent words spilling out of her mouth. Paul leapt off the chair and approached his wife. He quickly knelt down and firmly grabbed hold of her, pulling her into his arms. She was shaking and crying hysterically. Cleary was an experienced veteran of the force and reached into his pocket and placed a bottle of sedatives onto the table. He sat patiently waiting. Minutes marched on till Laura's crying turned into labored sobs. It was then that Paul scooped her up and gently placed her on the living room couch. The two men conversed quietly, and Cleary instructed Paul to hide the medication and administer it to his wife as needed. He handed him a business card and said he would be in touch and left.

The days that followed brought with them a combination of denial, anger, grief, depression, and loneliness. Then as they began to reconstruct their lives and work through things, they found acceptance and hope.

After the move to Cold Spring, Paul had opened a private practice, and Laura settled into the role of a stay-at-home mom. She spent her days gardening, cooking, and shopping. Since the murder, she had become withdrawn socially. She was a delicate flower, and Paul realized she just needed time, love, and patience, and he made every effort to provide her with daily emotional support. Weekends were devoted to a large variety of family excursions and overtime New York had become an insignificant, faded memory. Although Paul had kissed that life goodbye, he often found himself thinking of Annie. She bombarded his dreams, and occasionally a young girl's appearance or gestures in public triggered brief flashbacks of his daughter. Paul was not a religious or superstitious man, so had long written it off as a mild form of PTSD. A lot of marriages suffering their kind of trauma did not survive, but because of Paul's kindness and perseverance, they had beat the odds. His family was intact, happy, and content. Five years all small towns in America had basically remained unchanged. The fundamental aspects of farming and markets and a simple quiet life was flourishing. Now the larger metropolitan areas were a different story. Since the invention of computers by Steve Jobs and Bill Gates and the introduction of the Internet, subtle changes had taken place. Back in 1990, the online world had taken on a more recognizable form, when a computer scientist named Tim Berners-Lee invented the World Wide Web. By the year 2525, shopping malls and supermarkets had been replaced by distribution centers. Corporations that had not adapted to selling their produces solely on the Internet had ceased to exist. Companies focused on the laziness of society and had shifted the changing market to a home-based delivery system. Products were ordered online and either delivered by a distribution center or made available for pickup via a drive-through window. Places like gas stations and fast food restaurants were still around but converted to only a drive-through window. They had no need for a public seating area as they also focused on home delivery. Other changes had taken place, and the majority of the general population was either unaware or simply did not care. Public places, cars, and everyone's home had televisions and computers that monitored their every move. The government had many secret facilities that paid employees and trained them to observe people and regulate criminal behavior. Most of the general public was uncared about and simply a number of little importance to the government. The government also had eliminated all public assistance programs and had replaced them with free housing, food, computers, and televisions for all poor families. Some deemed these changes as productive and healthy and were oblivious to the real agenda of the government, for various reasons. Society had become slowly antisocial and isolated because of the WWW. You were deemed as weird or retarded if you made any kind of attempt to communicate or talk to others in public. The motto of society was absolutely don't talk to strangers for any reason. Schools were closed, and prisons changed to cloaked facilities that had slowly began to revise and shut down the current system. Inmates were tattooed, microchipped, and fitted with electrical bracelets. They were incorporated back into society because they were perceived as an undesired expense to the state and tax payers. Over time the new programs were intended to totally phase out the need for courts, judges, lawyers, and police officers. The convicts who were released and reoffended were instantly electrocuted to death and collected and disposed of. There was no trial by a jury of your peers; it was redundant because everyone was monitored.

As for the common citizen that committed murder, rape, or a crime against a child, they would be paid a visit at work or home by government officials who would take them to a secure facility and execute them and convert their remains to human fertilizer. No questions would be asked, and no answers would be given. All offenders would simply be shot. As for lesser crimes like speeding, a simple fine would be mailed, and as for consumption of alcohol, it would be strictly prohibited anywhere other than in private residential properties. Remaining bars would be shut down. Most of them had disappeared anyway because the malls all closed. School education and family counseling were offered online, and those that complied with the government regulations were issued financial rewards. All drugs were legalized and sold in stores, just like alcohol. The government cared less if people were wasted or even overdosed; they simple saw it as one less person to feed or monitor. As for impaired drivers, they did not exist because motor vehicles where equipped with high tech sensors that prevented them from starting if a person was drunk or stoned. Anything with a motor had them, so even boaters were stranded if they became intoxicated. Walking in a public place drunk or stoned was legal; in fact, the government found it amusing. The agency hired to monitor the public often watched impaired individuals with amusement. Newborn children were slowly beginning to be microchipped, and even street lights had night vision and thermal imaging devices installed. Homes not only had free television and computers to monitor people, the mirrors and lights fixtures in rooms such as bathrooms were also installed. Weapons were banned and considered illegal to own. The right in the states to bear arms was revoked and, over time, all guns would be seized and destroyed. Only appointed officials carried guns. In the wake of all the changes, the crime rate had slowly began to plummet by a small percentage in most states. The fulfillment of the public's basic needs of food, water, and housing, coupled with the new crime restrictions, would hopefully make it so people simply had no reason to commit illegal acts. Those that did would be dealt with discreetly and swiftly. As for sex, even prostitution was made a legal market that had home delivery. In large cities, you could get pretty well anything home delivered, thanks to the Internet. The system had many attributes, but it did have flaws; too many to mention. Sometimes wires got crossed and innocent people were executed, but the government saw this mistake as one less person to feed. The members of the agency also saw themselves as above the law and did not abide by some of the laws; but again, it was overlooked. It was swept under the rug and forgotten about. Some of the general population revolted. These people were quickly eradicated to prevent any civil uprising. Most of the fuss was over the right to bear arms since the general public knew nothing about the changes to the penal system. Now, again, don't forget that most of these changes were carried out over a span of years because humans are unpredictable creatures that are panicked by the unknown and change. The government had always lied to the public to a certain degree, so the changes they made in secret could be perceived as nothing new by normal standards. Most of the public was stupid, and again, oblivious to any corruption. It is easier to believe in words like *freedom* and *choice* verses *control* and *duress*. Most people exist in a little bubble and want to remain in it. Change introduced slowly is always embraced because people just don't notice it in most cases, or they follow the crowd, even if the changes are not productive.

The pilot program changing the educational curriculum to an online system was not a conspiracy or punishment. The government simply saw it as the next logical step for the evolution of learning. It was cost-effective, among other things. Problems like class volume were eliminated. Students were evaluated and received one-on-one attention according to their specific needs. Privacy made it so students doing poorly were not singled out or chastised by classmates. Discipline issues no longer existed. Parents were able to actively participate in their child's studies and were encouraged to do so. The service wiped out attendance problems because lessons were not limited or regulated by a set timetable. The user could log on twenty-four-seven, taking breaks at any time for naps, snacks, or playtime. Weather conditions and safety issues had become obsolete. Course selection was based on an academic review, and students moved along at their own pace based on their own ability. Individuals with disabilities were no longer faced with everyday mobility issues. Children as young as three could log on and play any of the large variety of readily available games geared to make learning fun. The dilemma of passing on childhood illnesses such as the flu or head lice was eradicated. Parents were overall less stressed and relaxed. The whole process had many positive attributes for taxpayers, government, and students of all ages. As an added bonus, a reward program was put in place where children were given t-shirts, gift certificates, bicycles, parties, and cash as an incentive to work hard and excel. Children were encouraged by the tutors to spend their free time using the Internet to research topics. Children were taught the Internet was a valuable tool with endless knowledge and information. This instilled healthy study habits and gave kids sense of self-worth and elevated esteem levels. Academically advanced students were required to log on less, and vice versa for the other end of the scale. The pilot program was a long, tedious job to convert all the educational institutions to online classes. The government started by closing schools with fewer pupils. Then they moved on to closing schools where children were bused in from other neighborhoods. The conversion was expected to be completed within a five-year period. In the beginning, some parents disagreed with the changes, but after realizing the many benefits and tax cuts, they adjusted and embraced the revisions. This deadline did not include the Mennonite community. Rural areas and small towns were still under review because small towns did not take kindly to outside interference.

The changes to the penal system that would take place in a shroud of secrecy were expected to be completed over a twenty-year period. A board of ten men composed of two scientists, five, high-ranking officers, two senators, and one court judge was selected. The ten men were chosen according to their individual abilities and their strong convictions about reform. They also needed to be trustworthy enough to maintain discretion during the course of the assessment. They had to prepare for and expect negative effects. Government choice would effectuate a transfer of responsibility of inmates from jails to society. An expanded breakdown of the list included an investigative scientist, a policy scientist, a lieutenant general, a colonel, a major general, a sergeant major, a command sergeant major, a New York senator, a Washington senator, and lastly, a district court judge. The order to form the committee was handed down from the Vice President of the United States. The order was the end of his involvement, the government wanted no briefs causing a paper trail. In the event of total disaster, the less people involved the better. The last member to join the team and appointed to oversee the project was a member of the Behavioral Analysis Unit. The men were ordered to work closely as a team; no leader was appointed, and the individual rank of the men had no bearing on how the team was expected to function. The BAU female appointed to oversee the project was the only female member of the team. The names of the team in no particular order were as follows: Jim McCormick, Jeff Raider, Marshall McKinnon, Ray Sanders, Melony Ashton, Scott Pearson, Mathew Stokes, Mike Wells, Robert Coldwater, Shaun Binder, and Jason Sparks. The team was instructed to wear normal clothes because they would invoke animosity within the jail population if they were dressed in military uniforms. The first six months in Auburn Correctional Facility located in Cayuga County, New York, were spent interviewing the 11,600 inmates. Although it was a long, daunting task, the eleven team members were at the top of their game and with their combined skills were more than qualified to cover every facet of the review process. Sergeant Major McCormick and Command Sergeant Major Sanders where part of the team for their innate ability to oversee the conduct and welfare of enlisted personnel. All five of the high-ranking military officers contributed great team work and leadership skills. Other skills included emotional resilience, physical endurance, practical intelligence, integrity, and discipline, not to mention their ability to follow instructions and make decisions under pressure.

Now, the investigative scientist Jeff Raider and policy scientist Marshall McKinnon were brought into the project for their ability to map, observe, monitor, and regulate data. The two senators, Mike Wells and Shaun Binder, also had solid organizational, leadership, and communication skills and both had bachelor's degrees in business and law to bring to the table. The last piece of the puzzle was district court judge Robert Coldwater. He was an active member of the Bar for five years, with active courtroom practice and had some litigation experience. His character traits encompassed his ability to apply patience, tact, firmness, open mindedness, and common sense to any debatable proposition.

CHAPTER TWO

It was the spring of 2030 and, surprisingly, it was a warm, balmy morning for a day in May. Paul woke early as the sun peered in his bedroom window. He did not get up immediately. He laid in bed, quietly collecting his thoughts and watching his sleeping wife. Although she had given birth to three children, she was still a stunning woman. She was five foot four and weighed about 140 pounds. She had long, poker straight, auburn hair and delicate, porcelain features. She could not be considered a spring chicken, but Paul still desired and loved her. He often found himself thinking what she really saw in him. He was not an ugly man, but his looks paled in comparison to hers. His height was six feet one inches, and he weighed approximately 230 pounds. His hair was jet black, and he had a clean-shaved face most days. His hair was beginning to recede, and his body was far from fit. It did not seem matter to Laura; she still eye-balled him like he was some young buck like Aaron Taylor-Johnson or Richard Madden. Over the years, many of their friends had divorced, but their marriage was strong and loving. Paul tried to slide out of bed quietly, but when he moved, Laura began to stir. Not once in twenty years was he able to successfully achieve this endeavor. It was as if she knew, even in her slumber, that he was not by her side anymore. He leaned and looked at her, and even though her eyes were shut, she smiled a big smile, and Paul began to laugh. He brushed her hair from her face and began kissing her as he gently whispered, "I love you, warden, but I need a pass. I really have to pee."

Laura stuck out her tongue at him and replied, "Well, okay, but hurry up. I can't have that side of the bed getting cold."

Paul smiled warmly and headed toward the bathroom. When he returned to the bedroom, Laura was sitting up in bed against the pillows, and he could feel her piercing, blue eyes studying his every move. As he gingerly rummaged through the dresser drawer, she spoke softly, "The warden says you are not allowed to get dressed yet." At this point, Paul began mocking her and repeating what she said over and over as he slid back in bed beside her. The boys had stayed over at a friend's place, and he knew they had the house all to themselves. He drew her close to him and kissed her hard. She gently sucked on his ear and whispered, "Does Mr. Simon intend to give Mrs. Simon everything she is paying for?"

With half a chuckle, he replied, "Honey, I can still give you a run for your money."

They exchanged no more words as Paul took her in his usual warm and tender fashion. Sometimes the science was off, but today, they were both in sync and achieved their peak together in a hot and sweaty climate. They both laid in each other's arms for some time before they finally rose and began their day. The house was peaceful and quiet, and Paul felt warm and content.

Laura was his best friend. Their friendship allowed for a strong bond between them. A friend is someone who knows your song and sings it to you when you have forgotten it. Those who love you are not fooled by mistakes you have made or dark images you hold about yourself. They remember your beauty, even when you don't. They make you whole when you are broken. They see your innocence when you feel guilty. He always felt purpose when he was confused. He valued their friendship. Over the years, their friendship paved the path for a strong and positive concurrent commitment. She loved him, despite all his flaws. She had a simple way about herself; an easy, laid-back manner. When they disagreed, she always said, "Let us talk and get to know each other. Where should we start?"

If he was to check all the boxes, they all would be yes. He adored her and counted on her. She brought him great comfort and touched his soul. She was his everything when he had nothing. She made him remember the awesome. She helped him to look on the bright side when he sat in darkness. She had never judged him by the scriptures of his faith or scars from his past. When he felt fear, outrage, and negativity, she helped him remain humble and kind. They were living proof that even through tragedy, people can still come together. She was his beautiful song, his addiction, his routine, and his emotional comfort. The days he projected darkness and had pain and internal struggles, she had nothing but kind words. She gave everything in her heart. He really believed her love was pure and had no limitations. He welcomed it.

Paul knew nothing for certain, but the sight of his wife gave him a star to dream by. After they dressed, they both decided to take the short walk to a local café for breakfast. The Black Forest Inn was a place they were familiar with, and the owners were friendly and kind. It was a carefree, long weekend, and the diner was a flurry of activity with a large amount of people enjoying a home-cooked meal. They both ordered eggs benedict, and as they ate, they enjoyed each other's company and conversation. Paul could not help but think how radiant and glowing his wife looked. As he gazed at her for a brief, fleeting moment, the thought crossed his mind that he had seen this look before. In the five years that Paul and Laura had lived in Cold Spring, they had made some good friends. The word friendship is not easily defined; it is a large spectrum of many opinions and ideas. Perhaps it is a person that stays in a moment of despair, confusion, bereavement, and the reality of powerlessness; a person that quenches your thirst for laughter, someone that stands by patiently and defends courageously, one who wishes you well for your sake alone, and a person in your life that is never to tired or busy. You fight for them, and they fight for you. A friend allows you total freedom to be yourself. They help relieve the gloom of your dark hour rather than enjoy only the sunshine of your prosperity. Some say we are born alone and live alone and die alone. Only through love and friendship can we create the illusion for a moment that we're not alone. Janet and Fred had been their next door neighbors for the entire five years since they had relocated, and over the years, they had shared many good and bad times. The first year after they settled in the small town, Janet had lost her new born daughter to SIDS. Laura and she bonded over the loss of the two girls. They shared a true, emotional connection.

A simple encounter while gardening had grown into a gentle closeness and comfort for both. When a man comes around, you feel safe and protected. Paul tended to focus on one thing at a time, though, and could not completely understand her feminine energy. When she acted like summer and walked like rain, Janet understood.

Paul could not help Laura the way Janet could. He loved his wife, but men don't, in most cases, deal with emotion in the same format as woman do. He had issues of guilt that if he would have protected his daughter better, the murder may not have happened. He had never totally shared his deep feeling with his wife; he just did not know how.

If Paul had to reflect, he really wondered where the years had gone. It was funny once you have kids how fast things seem to go by. Since the death of his daughter, he became a better husband and took a good, long, hard look at what he could do if he had the chance to do it all again. No one should have to bury a child. In the wake of death, we learn to cherish every moment and take not even a single breath for granted. Every day we hold them close and protect our child to the best of our ability, and then life takes a turn that is out of our control. His daughter's death left him angry. He remembered flashes of times they had spent together. It broke his heart. He wanted to drink to take the pain and memory, but he could not. He blamed himself. He found the strength to get off his knees. He could hear her say *I love you* like it was yesterday, and now she was gone. He missed her so much. Most days he felt like he was dreaming, hoping someone would wake him up. Her memory burned like a fire. He was crushed. He was afraid of moving on. He closed his eyes, and he could see her angelic eyes and soft smile. Pictures around the house reminded him. Her hair was so long, and he recalled the songs they sang in the car and birthdays. There was not going to be college or marriage for his daughter. He woke up many mornings from vivid dreams that left him scattered and feeling helpless. She had a place in his heart where no one had been. He wanted to be there for her first kiss and first true love, but that story was over. In a blink of an eye, her hopes and dreams where gone. He wanted to go down that road with her, but she was not around to take him there anymore; no sixteen candles for a birthday cake. Life is not always even what you think it should be, but it is grey when you have to bury your baby; a young girl that will never know the love of a man. In the end, you gather up your tears and put them in your pocket. They put her in the ground; they put her six feet down. They say time heals it all, but in Paul's eyes, it was bullshit. Time heals nothing. In the end, we just accept things not because we want to but because we have to move on. Contrary to popular belief, life is not about happy endings; it is more about just endings.

Paul and his wife were familiar with, and associated with, many of the town residents, but Janet and Fred were the only ones they classified as family. Laura also had hidden feelings regarding her daughter's death, but guilt was not one of them. She became systematic, going through everyday life with no meaning or purpose. She slipped into a darkness where going to bed had no reason and getting up had even less. She isolated herself and stopped eating. Her pain and despair ran deeper than anything, including tears, could fix. Even though Paul was a doctor, he was lost and did not know how to reach her or help her. The day she met Janet things slowly began to change for the better. The women found comfort through each other, and although Paul felt helpless, he also felt relief and comfort. Out of the ashes there was a new birth. The balance of life was restored, and Laura regained her strength and happiness. The memories of her daughter still lingered, but the pain no longer accompanied them. Perhaps it is true that we don't meet anyone by accident. Does the universe provide us with relationships that help us reach our life goals? We all look for reasons and answers. Maybe only through death can we truly understand living; not existing but living. When a man needs to see pure love, maybe only he can attain this by experiencing hate. Even the seasons are a subtle reminder that through the depths of cold and death, beauty and abundance are born. Adults forget this but watch a child experience winter or a rose for the first time.

It was around eleven when Paul and Laura finished up their breakfast at the café. They made the short walk home to find Janet at their door. Paul retired to his study to go over some medical files and left the women alone. The two women had plans to do some spring cleanup around the yard of the two houses and sip some wine and catch up on town gossip. Janet was sixteen years younger than Laura, but the two women got along very well. The age difference seemed to have little effect on their relationship. Janet stood about five feet five. She had wide set, small, dark eyes that were spaced evenly apart. Her jet black hair hung straight down into an angular cut at her jaw. Her features were accented by her apple cheeks, broad, rounded nose, and ruby lips. She had a kind of youthful glow and a lingering smile. As personalities go, she was adventurous, fearless, and charming. Laura had a more cultured, conscientious personality compared to Janet. Despite their differences, the two women had no difficulty spending numerous hours together and never tired of each other's company. Even though Janet was quite a bit different in age from Paul and Laura, her husband was not. Fred was a year older then Laura. He had rugged, sturdy features and a laid-back, calm personality. Fred had married Janet ten years back after he inherited his parents' hardware store after a freak car accident. She was his only family, and he loved her and took care of her accordingly. The loss of their child was horrible, but they recovered, and because of their friendship with Paul and Laura, they had the courage to try again. Janet was eight months pregnant and relieved to have Paul as a doctor and next door neighbor.

Out of the two thousand residents in Cold Spring, only six people had relocated to the town. The majority of the town's folk were born and raised in the farming community and surrounding area. Everyone identified others by the make and model of the vehicle they drove. Paul would always laugh and say the nice part about living in a small town was that when you don't know what you are doing, someone else always does. Rumors and gossip travel faster than lighting. It was definitely a slower paced life, and regardless of the gossip, Cold Spring had a sense of community. Life was simple with no distractions. Laura took great pleasure in sewing, baking, gardening, and walking the family's dog. The noise and chaotic life of their city life was nothing but a distant memory. The slower paced town was a great place to raise children. The boys, who now were thirteen and fifteen, had adapted to small town living and had many friends. Most evenings, after the boys had gone to bed, Paul and Laura would sit on the front porch and enjoy some wine and gaze at the night sky. They had never regretted the move to the small community; they only felt they had grown closer because of it. Life was tranquil and placid.

It was early Sunday morning at Auburn Correctional Facility. The inmates were eating breakfast and were scheduled for an orientation meeting to cover the components of the release guidelines. After the meeting, the board of ten men would each interview one hundred and sixty men individually to evaluate if they qualify to participate in the program. Low-risk offenders were granted an automatic release. These included anyone incarcerated for nonviolent crimes, such as drug possession, assault, careless driving, stalking, or maybe theft. Convicts who were serving back to back sentences for murder, rape, and pedophilia were considered violent offenders. An extensive review of violent offenders included risk assessment and security issues. The board looked at prisoner conduct, education, job experience, and social behavior of each inmate. Prisoners who had served most of their sentence and seemed somewhat rehabilitated would also be given a conditional release and monitored. Age was definitely a huge factor, along with mental stability. The majority of violent offenders would not be released, but instead, would be placed on death row and executed. Any men deemed narcissistic or incongruent with reality were considered too twisted to take a chance on. The members of the pilot program considered safety to be a top priority but also intended to release as many inmates as possible. If the mission was successful, they would release more convicts from other prisons. All inmates were expected to agree to every term and would be fitted with bar codes and electrical bracelets to make it possible for the board to monitor and maintain control over them. They were expected to keep in constant contact with their assigned program coordinator. Part of the terms included updated address and phone numbers and following rules and guidelines set up by the team.

Approximately ten percent of the prison population was considered too depraved and disturbed to put back in the general population and were dealt with accordingly. The majority of all violent offenders would never see the light of day, but five test subjects would. The study considered every possibility and outcome. The only fatal flaw was the illusion of control. In everyday life, we often think we can control other's actions, but this is a facade, we cannot. The only control we have is over our own actions. Perhaps the second mistake was to actually believe certain offenders could be rehabilitated. Even in the old system, many times inmates were released, only to recommit. It is one thing to be young and stupid and make mistakes and another to be some sick, disturbed person carrying out unspeakable acts. A child subjected to systemic abuse and deprived of basic needs in life generally cannot be fixed. No amount of therapy will fix or help them. Lack of love tends to breed hate. Most of us have bad memories in some form from our childhood, but we don't grow up so messed up that we harm others. In some form, we all carry baggage that effects our everyday life, but most of us let it go or learn to cope with it. Our parents inflict us with hurt and pain, and we grow up to pass this on to our offspring. In most cases, we don't even realize the damage we do to our children. Most parents do the best with what they have and understand. It is the parents that beat and abuse their kids that produce adults with psychological disorders that harm others. Some find the courage and strength to be productive members of society, and some just cannot. A child raised in a violent household generally grows up to be a product of their environment; the cycle is hard to break. Very few adults are born with issues; most are created by some kind of abuse in their youth. The first eight years of childhood form us for the rest of our lives. The Larson brothers were a fine example of parenthood gone wrong,

The Larson brothers were both arrested and put behind bars for armed robbery. No one on the board or in the prison system was aware that they had committed other crimes. Serial killers who slaughter random people quite often remain undetected for years. The boys grew up in a home where their parents beat and starved them. They were a classic example of offspring subjected to maltreatment and how it can derail a child. Early life conditions critically affect adult health. Maternal attachment plays a fundamental role in shaping who we are and what we become. Proper psychological and physical development requires nurturing and attention, not just food and water. The boys were isolated and neglected, which lead to addiction, distress, and many disorders. The end result turned into detrimental consequences for adults, the brothers were determined as bad people. They killed and dismembered the bodies and hung only the corpses' hands in local parks and placed them in mailboxes. They carried out this ritual to signify the hope and loving hands they felt they never had. The oldest brother, James, was a caregiver to his younger brother, Jeff.

One main reason the murders had gone undetected was because the two brothers were drifters who never stayed any place long. They lived in abandon houses and tents and hotels, when possible. The second reason was because they carefully disposed of the bodies and cut off the tips of the victims' fingers to conceal their identity. They also picked mailboxes and parks hundreds of miles from the murders. Many local police stations had hands but no bodies to go with them. The final reason was because both brothers had been captive for two years, so the murders had stopped. A lot of the rural homeowners did not even turn the hands in to the police. They might have been too scared or simply did not want to get involved. The police tend to look at in-laws as opposed to outlaws when a murder takes place, which also effects the chances of a serial murderer being caught. When someone kills a complete stranger, it quite often ends up never solved and ends up as a cold case filed on a shelf some place. Thousands of individuals disappear every year, and the bodies are never found. The board had no reason to suspect the two brothers of committing anything other than armed robbery and scheduled them for release. The two brothers were interviewed individually, and a psychological evaluation was never completed. The eleven, highly qualified team members had unknowingly opened Pandora's box. The project was expected do have issues, but this was a mistake that was about to unleash pure evil, carnage, and bloodshed to a countless number of innocent people who crossed the brothers' path.

At Auburn Correctional Facility, the team members slowly moved forward with the risk assessment review. Each inmate up for full parole was asked questions relevant to the crime. All convicts were asked to give facts and detailed versions of their offenses. Questions were asked about the inmate's behavior and plans and if they thought they had done anything to change. A review of the person's behavior while they were institutionalized was also conducted. The panel was looking for honesty, insight, and signs of remorse. Strict guidelines were set in place to ensure all convicts adhered to all the parole conditions. Any and all violations of the terms set up by the board would result in the cancelation of the parole, and the person would be dealt with accordingly. When Sergeant Sanders met Jeff Larson, he did not get any indication that he was vile or corrupt. His perspective was that the man was optimistic, quiet, and thoughtful. He did not seem anxious, depressed, or phobic. He did not pick up on the fact that James was egocentric and a dangerous menace. Sad part was he was completely fooled and felt an enormous amount of sympathy for the two brothers. When he read their case files, he learned that the boys were abused and abandoned at a young age. They were left to survive and support themselves. Sanders felt they deserved a second chance, so he signed off on the case and moved onto the next review.

Paul stood at the window and watched his wife and best friend cleaning up the yard. He felt so many emotions. He poured a stiff shot of Crown Royal and sipped on it. He did not drink much; he and his wife would be considered social drinkers, certainly not drunks. As he observed the women, he could not help think what they were talking about. Maybe it was kids or work or even him. Does a man really know the secrets a woman keeps in the depths of her heart? She needed him to love her, and he did. He hated most of her family, but he did not care what they thought or said; he had buried that demon long ago. They did not see them much; the boys knew his parents well but had little contact with her side of the family. Family is a funny thing that comes in many forms. Sometimes the people closest to us start out as strangers, and blood turns out to be our worst enemies. He held his head high; he did not care if he did not measure up to her parents' expectations. The death of his daughter had only made that worse. It gave them one more reason to cut him down, and he did not know how to make nice because he was mad as hell. In his eyes, family was supposed to support you, not put you down in a time of need. Toxic people have no right to infringe on people who want to move forward in life. Paul, most days, found himself blocking any memory of them. They had no right to take what he had. She was the one thing he could not stand to not have. After his daughter's death, he felt he was still paying the price. He just wanted to take care of her and put her on a pedestal. Her family resented him and did not treat him with any respect or decency.

Paul's family had enough money to be comfortable. Paul's father was an electrician and part of the working class. Laura's family was, on the other hand, filthy rich and were rude and obnoxious. They saw themselves as better than others; they had a huge sense of entitlement. Their level of wealth had seemed to decrease any feelings of compassion and empathy. Upper class and classy were a contradiction of terms for these people. Paul and Laura had met in high school, and he was nothing more than common trash from the beginning. His family was kind and generous because they knew what it was like to be poor. His father had never lost sight of where he came from. His parents were kind and loving and proud of their son's accomplishments. Laura was nothing like her family, and Paul thanked God every day that she was more like his parents. Everything she did she did for others; she seemed to get satisfaction from it, and many people adored her. As he watched them from the window, he had no idea that the two women were talking about Laura being pregnant and the best way to tell him.

CHAPTER THREE

Laura was very happy but a little apprehensive that Paul would not share her joy. She was worried he was still dwelling on the sting of the pain of losing their daughter. Sometimes life is not fair and has no guarantees. It is okay to have doubt. While Laura was busy getting stronger, Paul still seemed to be struggling with responsibility and how it correlated to his child's death. He kept rewinding the day she died and how he should have been there to protect her. The death of their daughter was a tremendous loss, but Laura thought it was time to overcome any obstacles and move on. She loved her child, and no parent should ever have to bury a child. She had no intention of tainting Annie's memory, but she wanted this baby more than anything in this world. Based on the advice of her dear friend, she planned on telling her husband that evening over a romantic dinner. She was not sure what his reaction was going to be, but she felt excited anyway. All through dinner, Paul kept asking what he had done to merit a fine meal, candles, wine, and romantic music. She just smiled a soft smile. It was after dinner when they retired to the porch to enjoy the enchantment of the evening sky that she sprung her secret on him.

Time had no meaning to Laura. Every morning she woke up early, and every day she still felt the sting of the pain, but she brushed her teeth anyway and got dressed through the mess and put a smile on her face. It does not happen overnight, but every day you get a little stronger. She knew her heart would never be the same. Even on her weakest days, she got a little bit stronger. She still cried whenever she thought about her daughter, but even though it was a broken happy ever after, she realized giving up led nowhere; no goodbye, no final kiss. The days were dark, but even in death, we somehow find life. Some believe God does not hand us anything we can't handle. If we embrace that the universe gives back what it takes, the baby was a rebirth and a second chance for them. Still, as we visit a gravesite, do we ever see it as fair as we move on with our own life? Young people are supposed to outlive their parents, are they not? We build our whole world around others, and when a child dies, we lose hope and question why. We question it even more when the parents have done nothing wrong but still the child dies. Hello, from the other side; we try to reconnect. It is not over for us, but it is for them. We need to believe, but the dead don't speak. In the silence, we think, *I am tired, I am lost, and I can't even say why.* The empty deep inside us says we are lonely still. She was New York born and raised, but the city was tainted with the bad memory forever.

It was a Friday afternoon, and the black Plymouth Duster had been parked out front the branded gas station for over an hour. The car likely went unnoticed as it was it was in need of some bodywork and had bald tires. It had a 360 Ci 4 Barrel V8 cylinder engine with automatic transmission and rear wheel drive. The 1970 Duster had seen better days but still ran strong and smooth. James and Jeff had been free men for less than a week but had already committed numerous offenses. They had robbed a homeless man, stole beer, and set someone's car on fire. The state had a clear fix on their location but no clue what they were doing or what was coming. For over a month, they drifted and stayed in cheap motels and spent their days drinking and vandalizing cars, parks, and abandoned buildings. They slept all day and carried out the crimes in the shroud of darkness. The Larson brothers were physically fit, with dark, curly hair and attractive features. They both were six feet tall, and other then a few, tasteless tattoos, no one would have suspected them to be vile, demented killers.

So, how many people do we meet in a lifetime? It could be a face-to-face exchange containing a clear, if momentary, recognition. It could range from a smile or a wave to a lifelong friendship. A 100,000, is that being generous? We could conduct a mathematical calculation and factor in such things as age, sleep, travel habits, the Internet, if a person is outgoing, and if someone lives in a rural town or populated city and even how many times we change jobs in our lifetime. The bottom line is we can't really calculate the number of people we meet and how many are unbalanced enough to be killers. Maybe it is your next store neighbor or the guy you're standing behind at a gas station or teller at a bank. Then again, perhaps, it is your wife or husband or son or daughter. Now take one step further and ask yourself if it is chance or fate that we meet and die or end up fighting for our life at the hands of one or two people out of that 100,000. It is kind of like winning the lottery, but not in a good way. So, three months later, when the Larson brothers settled in Cold Spring, was it chance or fate?

John Hopkins was an older male who owned a farm on the outskirts of Cold Spring. His kids had grown and moved, and his wife had passed on five years earlier. He had kept the farm because he was old and set in his ways and had no place else to go. It was a typical Saturday, and he was selling his eggs and produce at a roadside stand when an old Plymouth pulled up. The brothers exchanged friendly greetings and bought apples and tomatoes. It was typical, hot day for the middle of August, even though it was only noon. John repeatedly wiped the sweat from his brow as the men engaged in idle chit chat. Perhaps it was his attire or an idle comment that alerted James to the fact that the man was alone and somewhat of a recluse. It was in that moment that the older gentleman had sealed his fate. The two brothers conned the man into believing they grew up on a farm and loved fresh vegetables and farm fresh eggs. A simple, trusting gesture of inviting the two men up to his house to buy a few cartons of eggs was about to turn into the worst decision of his life. He had no reason to believe a few flats of eggs would cost him his life. John drove his old, beat up tractor up the half mile dirt road to his house, and Jeff and James followed in their duster. The pretty, white clapboard farmhouse had a wonderful wraparound porch with a traditional-style porch swing and two, pink rocking chairs. The roof was high with two chimneys that sat at either side of the house. Rows of small windows let in plenty of light to the rooms below the roof. The house itself was surrounded by a well-kept garden with scattered patches of various flowers and an enormous fountain containing koi fish in a small courtyard.

The two brothers lived in an imaginary reality that they created where only they existed. Trauma from their past caused them to create self-centered monsters as a defense mechanism. This monster was programmed to only care about their needs. The switch to caring and loving had been irreversibly turned off longtime ago. They had no healthy boundaries, and they literally had no stop button. They lacked any insight about how their behavior affected others. They were horrible men who had no regard for anyone whatsoever. They saw John as an obstacle to them having the house and land, and they intended to take the steps to achieve their goal of owning the property. The place was quiet and secluded and much better than the rundown motel rooms they had been living in. It was like a seaside hideaway and not even the agency would find them. It was two weeks and two hundred miles ago that they had cut off the bracelets and removed the chips from their arms. All that remained were the tattoos, and that could be passed off as bad ink. They had no clue why the bracelets briefly stopped flashing, and they did not care. They used the window of opportunity to cut them off and left the area. As far as the agency knew, they were still approximately two hundred miles west of their current location.

When a bee kills, it does this to protect the hive. When a lion kills, it does this to eat. When a man kills, he does it for sport, profit, and greed. Humans have no regard for the utopia they have been given, and they kill and pollute the earth. They view progress as constructing skyscrapers as a testimony to their success and leave their own kind on the streets to starve, sleeping next to buildings worth millions of dollars. Perhaps the Larson brothers were a product of society. Most of us are deterred by laws and consequences, but others are not, and the brothers followed only their own rules. Taking away their freedom and life was not even enough to stop them. In theory or on paper, it all sounds good, but in the end, they were just bad seeds killing only for profit and pleasure. Where are the dead? Are they aware of the living? Do the dead pass away to heaven or hell? Do we have immortal souls? Will we see deceased love ones again? The old man was about to find out the answers. If there was any. He gave them beer and lunch. They sat on the porch for hours, talking small talk, and he had no clue, no clue at all of what was to come. His dog had more common sense than him as she growled and avoided them. The old man paid no mind to her and carried on. It had been over a year since anyone paid attention to him or bothered to visit, so perhaps he welcomed the company out of loneliness, and this blocked his insight that they could not be trusted. Stupidity comes in many forms, and for many reasons, we trust for all the wrong reasons and dismiss our gut instincts because we want to believe people are loving and good. Even when his wife died and his kids moved away and had no contact with him, he still wanted to believe in the greater good; this would prove to be his downfall. He was about to learn the hard way to trust no one. What seemed like a normal Saturday was the day his life ended.

James and Jeff may have been related, but there were clear and significant distinctions between the two brothers. James was cool, calm, intelligent, and very manipulative. He was the most dangerous of the two because he was meticulous and planned things. Jeff, on the other hand, was prone to emotional outbursts and fits of rage. He was haphazard, disorganized, and spontaneous. His volatile nature was kept under control only because of James. One brother was a pure psychopath and the other a genuine sociopath. Only a sick and twisted man smiles as he tortures and mutilates a person. James enjoyed being up close and personal as he took his victims' lives. After his third beer, he politely asked John to use his bathroom, and when he returned, he had a butcher knife from the kitchen concealed in his pants and did not wait long to use it. In the fatal moment, the old man glanced over at him, not quite understanding why he was grinning. James reached behind his back, and in one swift motion, brought the blade down, cutting off the man's wrist, and before John had time to process what happened, he chopped off the remaining hand. Blood was squirting out everywhere. It did not take long before all three men were covered, along with the table and chairs and the porch floor. Jeff picked up the hands and began waving them and dancing around wildly. As the old man died, his face had a mixed expression of horror, fear, confusion, terror, and pain. James sat calm and motionless, still smiling.

The whole ordeal was over in under five minutes since the old man received no medical attention. His body flopped around and jerked as he bled to dead. The old hound dog had the good common sense to run off, but that likely would not help as the brothers intended to kill her, too. They figured she would attempt to dig up the body and would be a warning sign that the old man had not moved if kept, so she had to go. They did not stress or make any attempt to look for her; they figured instinct and hunger would make her return eventually. They buried the body in the backyard in the corn field and cleaned the blood off the porch. By the time they finished, it was dusk, and they entered the house to explore what the inside of the house was like. As enchanting as the outside was, the inside of the house was immaculate and luxurious. The generously sized living room had beautiful, mahogany hardwood floors and was graced by a fireplace and two, large, double-hung windows. It was a comfortable environment with an oversized sectional and a flat-top trunk as a coffee table. It also had two, floor-to-ceiling bookshelves and a patterned area rug. The kitchen was graced with stainless steel appliances, a large pantry, and a marble center island with seating. The crisp white cabinetry was accented by granite counters and his-and-her sinks. An oak staircase off the main entrance hall gave way to an oversized master bedroom, two small guest rooms, and two dream bathrooms. The huge master bedroom was stunning and sleek. It contained two, antique dressers, a wide-screened television, and a queen-sized bed. It also had glass walls framed in lovely laminate wood that gave the room a casual, relaxed feeling. French doors to the right of the bed opened to reveal a bright, stylish private toilet area with a wonderful free-standing tub. The decor included an old wine rack as a towel holder and two wall niches that displayed pretty soaps and vintage finds. The whole room had blue mosaic tiles and a lovely, zestfully clean atmosphere. The remainder of the upstairs consisted of two, smaller rooms with another full-sized, bright, stylish bathroom between the two of them. The only rooms in the house that appeared to have any sort of clutter were these two bedrooms. The first room had two, large bookcases with a wide variety of books. There was also a roll top desk in the room that was full of old papers, magazines, photos, and a computer. The second room was packed with a lot of boxes and old things such as lamps, toys, dishes, electronics, clothes, and antiques. Last but not least was the basement. It had a functional washer and dryer and a rustic wine cellar. It was windowless and dark and damp but a perfect place to store alcohol.

The basement had over four hundred bottles of wine and close to a hundred bottles of whiskey and fine bourbon. The collection of wines included cabernet sauvignon, zinfandel, pinot noir, chardonnay, sauvignon blanc, pinot grigio, and Riesling. The two most expensive wines in the collection were two bottles of Petrus, Pomerol 2002 from France, valued in the thousands. There were five bottles of bourbon whiskey worth fifteen thousand dollars. The rest of the collection was only valued at around a hundred dollars a bottle. The bottles were covered in dust and cobwebs, indicating they had been untouched for a long time. The rest of the basement had another rolltop desk and loads of antique furniture in very good condition. The forty acres of property also had a rather rundown barn with goats and chickens in it. Beside the barn was parked a black 2007 Honda Accord. The brothers moved it to the barn and covered it. They knew in the next few days they would have to drive it some place a long way from the house. They did not really know what to do with it. Maybe dismantling it was a better plan. James decided to sleep on it before deciding. The brothers settled in, cooked a late dinner, cracked open a bottle of bourbon, and drank the remainder of the night away.

CHAPTER FOUR

Some of us are born knowing what we want to be when we grow up. Some people figure it out later in life. Others wander through their lives perplexed, lost, and confused and never figure it out. Paul knew at a very young age he wanted to be a doctor and help people. Being a rural doctor was very rewarding. Paul and Laura had gotten to know a lot of the people in town because of his practice. He also had patients from Clayton and Sutton that bordered Cold Spring. Most of his patients were seen through appointments, but he did make the odd house call. He currently had four women in the family way, including his wife. Odd, his wife was not his first concern. He had experience, and people trusted him. He had a deep and compassionate bedside manner. He generally tried to stay out of family personal problems, but this was different. He was rather concerned about Molly Turner. She was sixteen and struggling. She was frail and young and had no family to support her. Her family did not care about her because they were too wrapped up in their own lives. Both her parents drank a lot and popped prescription drugs. All four of their daughters were neglected. She was scared and alone. When he looked at her, he somehow saw his daughter. He kept thinking, *What if this was my child?* The small town had no counseling services, so he chose to get his wife and neighbor involved. It was a simple act of kindness, woman helping woman. He figured his wife and best friend had more to contribute to her situation than a man or doctor ever could. His wife promised to spend time to relate to her during and after her pregnancy. Paul also applied for money from the state to help the young mother. His family knew about hardship and was more than happy to help the young girl.

It was a warm, summer day in the serene town of Cold Spring. Many of the town's citizens had gathered for a community picnic in Fall Kirk Park, just off Main Street. The event featured a few rides for the children and crafts and plenty of food. The town sheriff, Case Porter, and his young bride, Dixie, organized everything and even managed to find a few bands to entertain everyone. Paul and his wife arrived around noon and set up their umbrella and two chairs under a large oak, so Laura did not have to endure the hot sun beating down on her. It was a great day, sunny and hot with not a cloud in the sky. Paul arranged the small, red blanked they brought and placed their picnic basket in the middle of it. He gingerly unpacked two wine glasses and poured a half glass of red wine and handed it to his wife. As he leaned forward to steal a kiss, he heard a familiar voice. It was the eighth grade school teacher, Jade Meadows. She bellowed, "Get a room if you are going to be doing that sort of thing."

Laura yelled back, "Already have."

They all laughed and exchanged friendly greetings. Jade was an intelligent and very good looking blonde. Most of the time she loved to wear short skirts, and all the men in town sure did love to look. Today was no exception. She had on a black plaid skirt and a red halter top, and Paul could not help occasionally glancing her way. Every time he did, Laura smiled and swatted him. Finally, she whispered, "Stop! Damn, Paul, you are going to give me a complex."

Paul grinned and whispered back, "You lie, I am not."

She teased, "You're right," and leaned forward, put her arms around him, and gently kissed him on the cheek.

Jade had been single for around two years now. Her husband was an abusive drunk and had gambling issues. In the end, he had left her for another woman in Rio. She and her daughter lived in an old house just off Turner Road, not far from the public school where she taught. Everyone in town agreed she was better off without him. Plenty of men in town were willing to date her, but she just wasn't willing. Laura suspected she was enjoying all the new attention and was not ready to give it up by tying herself down. After all she had been through, who could blame her? Laura did not view her as any form of a threat. Paul was as loyal as an old hound dog and just liked to look. Some of the men in town might take it further, but not Paul. Out of all the town residents, Mia Harper was the only wife in town that had an unfaithful husband. No one could quite figure out why she put up with it. He dished it out, and she took it. They lived off Spring Street, and everyone in town knew John's reputation and often gossiped about who he was currently screwing. Some of the men at the local bar sometimes even made bets about it. They had a jar behind the bar for anyone interested in participating in guessing the woman of the month. All you needed was a ballot and ten bucks to get in on the action. It was not nice but a fact of life.

Small town living took some getting used to and was not for everyone. In a large city, gossip isn't as easy to spread with the volume of people, but in a small town, everyone knows everyone. Laura and Paul did not care; they viewed it as a minor issue compared to problems they had left behind in New York. The people overall were friendly and kind, and the crime rate was low, and that is all they cared about. The boys did not have to be on a short leash and had adapted to the freedom and had many friends. Laura spent most of her days preparing for the new baby. The boys both had their own room and an extra playroom now that they hardly used, so they had decided to convert that room to a nursery. Laura was far enough along to know the sex of the baby, but for some reason, Paul did not seem to want to tell her. In the beginning, she had nagged him but had given up assuming he had his reasons for not wanting her to know. As it turned out, Paul and Janet had planned a surprise baby shower and intended to gear the party according to the baby's sex. It was hard for him to keep it from her, but he knew, in the end, she was going to be so happy. The baby could never replace their daughter, but some of the sorrow would be a lot easier to bear when this new baby girl came into the world. Paul just wanted the whole experience to be absolutely wonderful. He wanted his wife to be fully content and happy. Janet was more than happy to plan the shower for her friend after the lovely shower Laura had given her five months back before her son Jake was born. Fred spent countless hours at the family hardware store, and it gave her something to fill her day. The two women also had a painting party planned to decorate the nursery for the baby. Janet was so happy for Laura. She and her friend were also planning a shower for Molly Turner and had adopted the young girl into their lives and hearts. Molly spent most of her time at Laura's house but also slept over at Janet's place. She rarely went home, and no one questioned it or blamed her. Laura liked to have her around; she was well-mannered and very pleasant. Both families helped her with clothes and made sure she adopted some proper habits regarding nutrition. Paul supplied her with free prenatal vitamins, and everyone helped in any way they could.

As the sun dwindled and most of the families had gone home, ten volunteers stayed to clean up the park. It was among the scattered trash that one male named Howard Johnson made the gruesome discovery. Under some discarded chip bags and Coke cans was a set of hands clearly cut off near the wrist. At first he stared at them in disbelief, and then he called two of the other men close to him to have a look. The three men were shocked and revolted and exchanged some swear words before sending someone to get the town sheriff. Case Porter instructed no one to touch them and sent everyone home immediately. The park had just become a crime scene, and he was worried it was already contaminated and valuable evidence had already been lost. There was no way of telling at this point how long they had been there and how many people had trampled over them. That park had over five hundred people in it over the course of the day. The first thing he did was call the coroner and had his men tape off the area. He had many questions, and at this point, ruled out no one. He sure hoped it was not one of the members of the town, but at this time, had no way of knowing for sure. The first step was to let Greg Farrow examine the hands. It was about an hour before Greg arrived on the scene. Case was sitting at a nearby picnic table, taking notes and trying to decide his plan of attack. He knew the three men would not keep silent long, and the news would spread like wildfire. He was concerned that gossip would hinder his investigation. When Farrow approached, he pointed at the hands and sat patiently waiting as he watched him put on a set of rubber gloves and bend down to take a close look the severed hands. Greg began to shake his head and then he spoke, "Christ, Case, this is a family park. What kind of fucking animal leaves hands in a family park?"

Case replied, "Yes, Greg, I share your distain, but what can you tell me about them?"

"What I can tell you is they are clearly female, but till I get them back to the morgue, I cannot determine if there is enough of the fingerprints to tell us who they belong to."

As he put the hands in a plastic bag, he explained to the sheriff that he would phone him in the morning with any details he could uncover, and then he left. Case had his men check the park and its perimeter for any obvious evidence, and then they called it a night. He had two cruisers stay behind to monitor for any intruders. He wanted the park kept empty for the night. He also wanted the park watched on the off chance the perpetrator happened to return. He was tired; it had been a long day that had ended badly. He went home to his wife and kids and tried to relax with a couple of stiff shots.

It was 7:00 A.M., and Case Porter was awoken by the sun shining in his bedroom window. He could hear the muffled sounds of his children coming from what he assumed was the kitchen. He had no desire to get up and face the day. It was a small town where nothing ever happened. He knew yesterday's discovery in the park was about to change that. He was not even sure about what route to go. He had two choices: to interview the entire town by going door to door, or call a town meeting. After his morning coffee, he picked up the phone and called the coroner. The only thing Greg could tell him was the hands were female and approximately two days old. There was no viable fingerprints to identify who they belonged to. Greg informed him he would preserve the hands and suggested they might have to call in a forensic pathologist from out of state. Case hung up the phone and sat sipping his coffee and shaking his head. He knew eye witness testimony was very unreliable and more than likely would not shed any light on the situation. The biggest question he kept thinking about was where the hell was the rest of the body. As he sat pondering it, his wife served him some scrambled eggs and toast. She said, "Case, do you think you are going to find the rest of that poor girl's body?"

Case responded, "Well, honey, at this point, that definitely is one of my biggest questions.

What worries me is that we will find it."

He finished his breakfast and did not say anything else to his wife. He had no desire or intention of sharing the one thought that concerned him the most. What kind of a sick bastard dismembers a body? He put his dishes in the sink, kissed his wife goodbye, and headed for the office.

After a brief consultation with his deputies, Case decided to post an advertisement in the local newspaper and to individually interview anyone he thought might know something. The article the paper published ran right away in the evening addition. It read as follows:

POLICE ARE LOOKING FOR ANY EVIDENCE REGARDING THE REMAINS FOUND IN FALL KIRK PARK EARLY THIS WEEK. COLD SPRING POLICE ARE URGING ANYONE WITH ANY IMPORTANT INFORMATION TO COME FORWARD OR CONTACT CASE PORTER 209-555-6565 EX. 403. ANYONE WISHING TO REMAIN ANONYMOUS ARE INSTRUCTED TO LEAVE A DETAILED NOTICE IN THE MAIL DROP BOX OUTSIDE THE TOWN PRECINCT. A FIVE THOUSAND DOLLAR REWARD IS BEING OFFERED FOR ANY TIP THAT LEADS TO AN ARREST AND CONVICTION OF THE PERPETRATOR OF THIS CRIME.

The following morning the calls began to pour in, but most of the tips were useless information and inquiries about what was found. Case was frustrated and empty-handed. In the weeks to come, the department rounded up one hundred volunteers to organize a search of the town and the surrounding wooded area. Case recorded the names and contact details for all the volunteers prior to them embarking on the search. No one under the age of eighteen was allowed to participate. The large group was divided into smaller groups of eight to ten people. The teams were given a list of items to bring to the foot search. These included walking sticks, boots, first aid kits, whistles, water, a camera, sunscreen, cell phones, and brightly colored tape. Case got maps of the area and separated them into grids and appointed one person in each team to be the map holder. Everyone was instructed to go slow and look at their surroundings. They were told if they came across something suspicious to tag the area with a piece of the bright yellow tape. The groups were told to not touch anything that could be evidence and to be mentally prepared and alert at all times. They covered fields, cliffs, ditches, and even the trees.

On the fifth day of the search, two volunteers came across a clearing in the woods just east of town. In the middle of the area were the remains of what looked like an old hound dog with its insides torn out. All the trees on the outskirts of the clearing had bloody, dirty clothes tied to the branches. Hundreds of pants, shirts, and shoes of all sizes were strung up. It looked like some sick attempt to mimic a Christmas tree; only whoever made it used bloody clothes instead of balls. The area was cordoned off, and everyone was sent home. Case and his officers took photos and bagged and tagged everything, including the dog. After everything was transported to the morgue, the men returned to the precinct, where Case called an emergency meeting. Normally they would not have been permitted to drink on the job, but Case made an exception and ordered in some food and alcohol for his men to consume. It had been along and stressful week for all involved, but Case needed to review the bizarre findings while the information was still relatively fresh. After Case instructed everyone to absolutely not share any details of the case, they moved on to discussing any questions and insights they all might have. The first to speak was Lieutenant Gordon Holdings. He pointed out that based on the height and position of where the clothes were, it was more than likely a male suspect or suspects. He also mentioned that he felt they were experienced killers because of the attention they paid to detail and the lack of incriminating evidence. Everyone concurred. The one question on everyone's minds was, *Where the hell was the body to go with the clothes?* They had dug and excavated the whole area, and not one, single body part was recovered. Late into the night, the officers drank and mulled over the aspects of the case. As the night progressed, they packed it in and spent more time drinking and socializing than doing any work. Case understood they needed to blow off steam and did not shut the party down. Case planned in the weeks to come to monitor everyone in town closely and to also Look for and scrutinize any newcomers to cold Spring . He could not rule it out but was pretty sure it was not anyone that lived in the town. If it was, signs would have showed up before now. Whoever these sick bastards were, he was fairly confident they were outsiders. He did not want to alarm or panic people, but he was absolutely positive this was far from over and about to get way worse before it got better. One thing he was sure of was he was not going to give up until these sick fucks were dead or in jail. The following week, when another set of hands was found strung up in a tree in Fall Kirk Park, Case placed a call out of state to an old friend.

Captain Coop Macy was an experience veteran of the NYPD, and Case trusted his judgment. When Case finally got Coop on the phone, he explained the odd set of events that was going on in Cold Spring. He said, "Christ, Coop, it is the craziest shit I have ever come across. I got two pairs of severed hands and no leads. I need your help."

Coop assured him he would be there by that afternoon. Case thanked him and hung up the phone. Case took a half hour to make sure all the evidence was intact and neatly compiled in the conference room for the captain. When he decided everything was satisfactory, he slipped out for coffee across the street. The café was packed with the usual patrons, and everyone eyeballed him the minute he stepped through the door. The whole town wanted answers. Everyone was on edge and afraid to walk the streets after dark. The whole affair was downright creepy. Case understood their concerns, but he was not at liberty to share any of the details of the case with anyone. He did not even get a chance to place his order before people started shouting at him and demanding answers. He sighed and quietly began to speak, "Look, folks, the whole force is monitoring the town twenty-four-seven. The best thing right now is to remain calm and let us do our jobs. Past that I got no information to share with you at this time."

The last comment he made was to inform everyone that no one was to even consider taking the law into their own hands or they would find themselves in cuffs. He grabbed his coffee and left. As he slowly crossed the street, he thought, *Fuck me, they don't pay me enough to put up with this shit.*

Coop Macy arrived in Cold Spring, and he wasn't alone. He was accompanied by a homicide detective and a forensic pathologist. Coop assured Case that they were not there to pull any out-of-jurisdiction crap that the plan was to work as a team and resolve the crisis. Case was relieved to have their help and hopeful it would speed the investigation up. After the three men did a quick review of the work Case's department had completed, they agreed that they all had done a very fine job. They had documented everything and nailed down a timeline and preserved the evidence like they should have. They definitely could see what they were up against since there were no fingerprints, DNA, murder weapon, or complete bodies to go by. The only thing they could all do at this point was take witness statements and follow any leads, no matter how small they were. They hoped if they were patient, something would turn up, so they could bring the perpetrators to justice. At this point, all they could do was watch and wait and continue to document the clues. Case got the three officers set up in the local bed and breakfast and then he and his friend went for drinks at his home. Over a beer, Coop told his friend not to stress; he guaranteed him that the idiots would screw up eventually and leave an incriminating piece of evidence to nail them. He reminded Case that for now, their best bet was to look for any eyewitnesses. Coop Macy had solved many murders, and for him, this was a walk in the park. He knew patience was the key. The rest of the evening the two men talked about old times and enjoyed each other's company. Three weeks passed, and two adults and a ten-year-old girl showed up at the precinct. The little girl had seen a black car sitting on the street by Fall Kirk Park. She did not know enough to get a license plate, but she did tell Case the two men were tall with dark hair. It was not a lot, but it was something. He gave the young girl fifty dollars and thanked her parents for bringing her in. The little girl smiled, and Case told her she was a real hero; that seemed to make her proud she had come forward. Two more months passed without any leads, and Case was beginning to worry that the whole ordeal was going to turn into a cold case file. It was then that things took a turn for the worse! A young woman named Molly Turner was reported missing.

Case was not sure if he should take the matter seriously because Molly's parents were totally inadequate, and half the time they had no clue where any of their children were. These days he knew she spent most of her time at Laura and Paul Simon's place. When her parents phoned the police precinct, he would have told them to call the doctor's house, but he did not really want to get involved in the middle of a family squabble. At 10:00 A.M., when Paul and Laura walked into the office, it was then that he had cause for concern. After a brief interview with the couple, he issued a statewide Amber Alert for the girl. Laura told Case that Molly was happy and had no reason to run off, and that was good enough for Case. Posters were put up all over the town, but no one seemed to know anything. A day later, the town rallied together and formed a search party. They combed the entire town and ten miles around it. Nothing was found. Laura was extremely stressed and not sleeping. Paul decided to administer her a mild sedative because he was worried about the baby. Paul's feelings of helplessness and inadequacy returned, and for the first time in his life, he got completely drunk and passed out on the porch swing. At 3:00 A.M., he was awoken by the barking of his neighbor's dog. His head was pounding, and as he staggered to his feet, he noticed a tall man with dark hair standing in his driveway. Thinking he was hallucinating, he ignored what he saw. He entered the house and slept the remainder of the night on the living room couch.

The following morning, Paul woke to the aroma of fresh brewed coffee and got up and headed for the bathroom. He had a splitting headache and was rummaging through the medicine cabinet for aspirin when his wife came up behind him. She was holding a cup of coffee, and he was grateful. He grabbed the aspirin bottle, and they both headed for the kitchen and sat down at the table. They sat in silence for over five minutes before Laura began to speak. She spoke softly, "Honey, I know your hungover, but we have to talk. I know our family had been through hard times before, but this time is different. I feel it in my soul.

"Paul, you and I are struggling, and I cannot function if I have to worry if the boys are safe. Paul, don't be angry. I think it is best for all of us if we send the boys to New Jersey to your parents' place for the time being. I already called them, and they agree it is the best idea for all involved."

Paul looked at her with a blank stare, and even though a man is not supposed to cry, he began to weep. As she stood by his side with his head in her hands, kissing and consoling him, he spoke, "Laura, I want you to go with them. You don't want the boys in harm's way, and I don't want you and the boys and the baby in any danger, so you're all going. Baby, this time around, we have the chance to take precautions, and I will be okay. "You're all going, and that is that," he announced.

She had never been far from her husband's side, and she did not want to go, but she smiled and agreed. The next morning, she and the boys packed and left for New Jersey. Paul felt like his heart was ripped from his chest, and the house was so quiet you could have heard a pin drop. It was okay, though, because relief overpowered the loneliness he felt. He still dedicated his time to his medical practice and spoke to Laura every evening on the phone.

Many of the other residents of Cold Spring had the same idea, and the place became a virtual ghost town. Mostly all the families sent their kids to relatives' houses till things cooled down. Just when everyone thought the worst was over, another set of hands and partially formed fetus was found in a shoe box in Paul's roadside mailbox. Within twenty-four hours, the coroner this time determined it was the remains of Molly Turner and her baby. The hands did not have the fingerprints cut off, and the DNA from the fetus, when matched with her parents, clearly established it was Molly's baby. The following morning, the rest of Molly's remains were found in Fall Kirk Park. Case was angry. It was like the suspect was mocking him and his deputies. A few pairs of hands were one thing but finding the remains of Molly was up close and personal; the sick bastard was either coming unraveled or he was making fun of the town. The body of the young girl was totally divided up. The head was decapitated and displayed with makeup on her face, and the body parts were placed in order, within one inch of the skeleton. Every organ was fully intact, and little blood was found on the scene. The corpse had no skin, but the remains were lined up like a human jigsaw puzzle. Thousands of flies covered the body. Case had a hard time keeping his breakfast down. He covered the body with a tarp out of the back of his Jeep and sat down and again waited for the coroner. After the remains were removed, the whole park was taped off, and huge, wooden signs were nailed up forbidding anyone and everyone from being in the park. As the men watched Greg load the body in the back of the forensic van, they discussed their options.

Case stood eyeballing his men with an angry scowl on his face. The park had been under supervision every single night for a month, and he wanted an explanation why this fucker had slipped by them. He did not even realize he was shouting until Coop gently put his hand on his shoulder. Coop said, "I know you're upset and frustrated, but this won't solve our problems. Here is what I am going to do, Case. I am going to make some calls and get a hundred officers sent here from the NYPD. We will put them in plain vehicles day and night all over town and see if we can flush this fucker out. I will instruct them to use no headlights at night and remain as invisible as they possibly can. We will also discreetly place cars near the two highways coming into Cold Spring and monitor every single vehicle coming and going."

Case shook his head yes and also suggested they put plain-clothed officers in the bar and local gas station. Coop smiled at the other officers and said, "Okay, men, time to put an end to this game of cat and mouse. Let's take this fucker down." They assigned an officer to every single family that was willing to let them come into their home, and everyone stopped wearing police uniforms and dressed in street clothes. They made every attempt possible to hide in plain sight.

CHAPTER FIVE

All the men in Cold Spring were beginning to show signs of being distraught and anxious. On more than one occasion, the police had to break up violent outbursts that broke out at the local pub. Some were because of alcohol, and some were not. Case was beginning to lose his patience. Case had joined the police academy straight out of high school and had been a sheriff in Cold Springs for about ten years. He was thirty-four years old and stood approximately five feet eight inches. He was not what you would call an attractive man, but he did have a charming personality, and that is what had landed him his pretty wife. Over the years, he had let himself go a bit and was overweight for his height. Like most men, the extra weight was all in his midsection. His wife, Sarah, had tried many times to put him on a diet and finally gave up, deciding it was futile. Case was a meat and potatoes man and did not take kindly to having a salad put in front of him. He also enjoyed a few cold ones after his shift. He was a dedicated, hardworking man and felt he deserved a few drinks after work. Sarah never complained, but hard liquor was not permitted in her home, and she was adamant about it. Only on very few occasions had she allowed it, such as when they had family by at Christmas and Thanksgiving and now, since Coop was visiting. She knew Coop drank rye, and she was not about to embarrass her husband in front of his friend. Sarah was a quiet, well-mannered woman, and she loved Case, despite his flaws. They only had the one son, Cory, who was now six. They wanted more kids, but she got cancer and had a hysterectomy, which put an end to that dream. She always tried to stay positive, so she always reminded Case one was better than none. She did tend to be a little overprotective because he was an only child and still pretty young. Like everyone else in town, they had sent him to California to her sister's place to protect him from the impending danger. Sarah rarely drank but was uptight as everyone else and joined the men on the porch for a few drinks that evening. The moon was full, and the stars were bright, and she tried to focus on that and the conversation to help the pain she felt in her heart because her son was gone.

She was also on sedatives that Paul Simon had prescribed for her, and she was not the only one in town taking medication from the good doctor. The situation was like something out of a horror movie. Case rarely spoke about any problems about work, but this time was different. It definitely was a hot topic. After they consumed steak and potatoes prepared on the barbecue, the two men engaged in a spirited exchange of ideas and views about the whole affair. Case was apprehensive about the hundred extra officers to supervise, but Coop told him to let him worry about controlling his staff. He told his friend they had bigger problems coming. He explained to Case that if they could not keep the news media out of the locality, the whole case was going to end up in the toilet. Right now, they had the upper hand because the perpetrator had no clue what they knew or what they were doing. The media would ruin everything. Coop hated reporters; he saw them as blood sucking vultures. If the media showed up, they would likely spook the man, and he would disappear; or, to make matters worse, feed his ego, and the murders would likely escalate as a result of it. Both scenarios would end as a no-win situation. He also reminded Case that time was not on their side. They were running out of time and needed answers now. The people in the town wanted results, and families could not keep their loved ones gone forever. Another issue was money. Cold Spring' budget to pay its officers was stretched thin to begin with, and soon he would be paying his men with buttons if they did not solve this thing soon. As the two men sat on the porch and consumed alcohol, the two men agreed the whole affair was deeply unsettling. When Case finally retired for the night, he could not sleep. Every time he closed his eyes, all he saw was the body parts in the park. He finally took one of his wife's sedatives and woke the next morning around six.

On the other side of town, Paul Simon was not coping any better. He was convinced he was coming unhinged. He was having trouble getting to sleep, and when he did, he was plagued with constant nightmares. He repeatedly saw gruesome images of Molly Turner. The slain girl was standing in a field beside a rundown barn. Blood was seeping out her nose and eyes, and she was whispering the same macabre message over and over again: YOU HAVE SEEN HIM, PAUL! YOU HAVE SEEN HIM! He had not told Laura about the discovery in the mailbox or the unsettling dreams. She had been through enough, and he did not want to burden her. When the sheriff had picked up the remains, Paul made it clear his wife was never to be told anything about it. Nothing good could ever come of his wife and kids knowing. The long days and lonely nights were making Paul even more unraveled. He wanted to temporarily close up his practice, but they had bills to pay, and the residents of the town needed him. When he lay in bed at night, he could always hear the freight train passing through Cold Spring. In the distance, the engine moaned, and the whistle blew, and a blue melancholy feeling crept over him. He always imagined it was a midnight train bound for nowhere and wondered why it always made him feel so down. He was not a man to dwell on emotions, but the absence of his family was starting to bother him. He decided to take three days off and take the ten-hour trip to New Jersey. It might have been a long drive, but he did not care. He left the following Friday, bright and early at the crack of dawn. He arrived at his parents' house around six that evening. They were just sitting down for dinner, and Paul was starving and happy to have a home-cooked meal. His wife and mother smiled at him and he uttered "what" as he shoveled the food in his mouth. His mom let out a laugh. "Paul, you're acting like you have not eaten in a month."

Laura began to roar as she announced, "Nancy, have you ever tasted his cooking? I swear the man could even burn water." At that point, even Paul began to chuckle. He might have been a brilliant doctor, but his cooking truly did suck.

It was not till later that evening when the boys were in bed and the family was having a night cap that Paul's mom mentioned her concern. Paul did not want to make light of the situation, but he did not want to create panic, either. He calmly explained to his parents it could happen anywhere and not to worry, it was under control. His mom dropped the subject, even though she could see anguish in her son's eyes. His dad reminded him that if he needed anything, they were only a phone call away and then changed the subject to talking about the weekend. He suggested that they all should go to Liberty State Park for a family picnic. Paul was happy and content. He wished he did not have to go back and that his goddamn house would burn to the ground while he was gone. He could not even sell the fucking thing at this point; no one in their right mind would purchase it. If he closed his practice, they would lose the house and everything they had worked for. That night when they went to bed, Paul wanted to tell his wife what had happened; instead, he lied and told her Molly had not been found. They made love, and Paul drifted into a deep sleep. At 3:00 A.M., he was awoken by a vivid dream of Molly's bloody hand shaking him and screaming, YOU KNOW WHO HE IS! HELP ME, YOU KNOW WHO HE IS!" It took him a moment to realize it was his wife's hand shaking him.

"Paul," she whispered, "are you okay? Honey, you were yelling in your sleep."

He stared blankly at her and then quietly apologized. She held him and kissed him, and they lay back down together. He smiled at her, but she knew he was hiding something. She was a lot of things, but stupid was not one of them. She smiled back and snuggled close to him and listened to his breathing and drifted back to sleep. Paul lay still, watching his wife and feeling her warmth and managed to drift off again, too.

The next morning, Laura managed to slide out of bed without waking her husband. As she and his mother had tea, she told Nancy about the disturbing nightmare. She said, "It was the darndest thing, Nancy. He was yelling over and over, 'You know who it is.'"

The only advice his mother had for her was to love him and comfort him while he was going through this crisis. The two women lovingly prepared him breakfast in bed and worked hard the whole weekend to pamper him. His mother explained he would share the problem when he was ready, and Laura trusted her judgment and left the issue alone. Summer was in full swing, and the whole family enjoyed a glorious day at the beach. Afterwards, they all dined out at a fancy steakhouse and enjoyed an evening stroll along the boardwalk. They arrived home shortly after dark and retired on the porch for their usual nightcap. Laura tucked the boys in bed and joined the rest of the family. As she sat beside Paul, he lovingly rubbed her stomach and gently took her hand. The moon was full, the sky was crystal clear, and the stars twinkled like huge diamonds. Paul sat quietly, sipping his whiskey, when he suddenly had a flashback of the man standing in his driveway. Not really realizing it, he stood straight up and dropped his glass, and it smashed as it bounced off the wooden floor of the porch. He was stumbling around franticly until his father grabbed him and forced him to sit back down in his chair. He held him tightly until he began to calm down. Nancy and Laura both had stunned, horrified expressions on their faces. Paul's father looked shocked and angry. He looked at his son with a stern expression and said, "Okay, Paul, what the fuck was that? We are aware of what is going on with you, and it ends here. You are going to come clean, and you are going to do it now. Sometimes, son, you can't go it alone. The only way we can help you is if you tell us."

They all sat completely silent as Paul explained in detail the whole, sorted tale. The last thing he said was about the night he had been drinking and saw the tall man with dark hair standing in his driveway. He looked at them and swore, "Dad, the fucking son of bitch was standing in my driveway, watching me. The fucking jerk was staring directly at me."

Tim instructed his wife to get him a new drink, and he calmly told Paul he was not going back home alone. "Together we will deal with this, son. Together you and me and your family will be safe here." Paul looked at him and nodded his head yes. He was still shaking but managed to calm his hands enough to belt back the whiskey. The woman went to bed, and his father and he sat on the porch for a good portion of the night before they finally turned in. The dream never returned.

When Monday morning came, Paul was sad to leave his wife and kids behind but took solace with the fact that they would be completely safe. He and his dad packed up the sedan and ate breakfast, and then they left for Cold Spring. They arrived late and were very tired, but Paul called the sheriff's office anyway. A young rookie answered the phone and patched him through to Case Porter's private line. Paul explained the circumstances to him, and Case instructed him to come in first thing tomorrow morning. Paul agreed to the meeting and hung up the phone. He got his dad situated in the guest room, and the two men cooked dinner and enjoyed a few beers. Paul thanked God for his dad's company and that his dad could cook. He felt relaxed. That night he slept like a baby, just knowing his dad was in the house. The next morning, he and his dad went to the precinct, and they sketched a composite of the man and had Paul leaf through a book of mug shots. Case thanked him, telling him it was a valuable lead. They knew what he looked like now, and that he was watching everyone in town. He also told Paul plain clothed officers in unmarked cars would be monitoring his house day and night on the off chance he showed up again. Paul shook his hand, and then he and his father left. They crossed the street and ate breakfast in the local café. Paul informed his dad he did not have to accompany him to the office, but his dad followed him anyway. Paul laughed and reminded his father he was married and to not flirt too much with the female patients. Tim slapped him on the back and told his son he would try to behave. It was a slow day, and Paul closed up the office early.

After Paul Simon left, Case and Coop sat down and reviewed the eyewitness account. Coop was concerned about the quality of the artist's hand and Paul's memory retrieval process. Coop explained to his friend that their witness's recall memory needed no priming, but his recognition memory took its cues from different parts of the brain and may be affected by stress, trauma, and time lapse. The recollection could be muddled. Depending on the circumstances, a criminal's face may never make it through the brain's memory-making process. To store a memory lock-tight, the brain must encode a face, consolidate all of the information about that face (eyes, nose, facial hair, etc.) and catalog it alongside similar-looking faces already stored in their brain. The hand-drawn sketch had about a nine percent accuracy rate. Case looked at his friend and started to shake his head. He told Coop he loved him, but he did have a tendency to overanalyze everything, and he needed to lighten up. He suggested they fax the sketch to the NYPD and compare it to their mug shots and run a criminal record search and see if they got any hits. Coop told him to politely go fuck himself but agreed.

The following morning a fax came in regarding the sketch. It was two mug shots of two brothers, Jeff and James Larson, convicted of armed robbery two years back. Coop stood scratching his head. Everyone in the precinct agreed some kind of mistake had to be made. No way would two criminals convicted of armed robbery would be released in a period of two years. One of the rookies who had been sent down from New York overheard the conversation and said it was possible. His name was Steve Bender and he had only been on the force six months. Coop shot him a look of disapproval and walked away. The boy followed him to his office and politely asked for five minutes of his time. "Please, sir," he insisted, "I know what I am talking about. Please give me the chance to explain." Coop was not impressed but decided to indulge the rookie and instructed him to come in and sit down and slammed the door behind him. The kid proceeded to tell him a story about his older brother, Sam, who had been a prisoner in Auburn Correctional Facility. His brother had been convicted of fraud and was serving a five-year sentence and was released six months ago. Coop looked at him like he was a fucking idiot. The boy continued anyway, "My brother told me, sir, they are conducting some kind of a secret program there and releasing everyone but violent offenders." Coop told the young rookie that fraud was a long way from armed robbery and maybe his brother was out because of good behavior. Steve insisted it was not good behavior and told Coop if he did not believe him he could bring his brother into the precinct. Coop was not sure what to think. The whole story seemed rather thin, but he decided to have the brother come in out of sheer, morbid curiosity.

If there was any amount of truth to the rookie's story, it likely meant the mug shots were not a mistake. It also meant that his force had stumbled onto something that the FBI or the government or both wanted to keep a lid on. It was not something Coop Porter wanted to be in the middle of, but he also had no intention of letting these two, sick bastards continue their reign of terror. If they were the right killers, they were going to be caught or killed, and Coop did not care which. The brother did not come into the precinct, but he did contact Coop by phone. He assured him Greg was not deceiving him, that the prison was indeed conducting something they called a pilot program and granting early release to all the prisoners that qualified. Coop could not believe his ears and was totally appalled that these state officials and their bureaucratic bullshit had caused this problem. Two men that should still be behind bars were free and killing people because some asshole had made a horrific mistake. He was angry, but it did not change anything, regardless of how it happened it had happened. The task at hand was finding the two brothers. Knowing who they were was one thing, but locating them was an entirely different matter. He and Case had no leads except the good doctor. They continued to watch his house and decided that the mailbox gift might be a valuable clue. Case ordered his men to check and recheck every mailbox in town and the surrounding area. They also decided to dust Paul Simon's mailbox for prints. It was just a formality since they were sure it was the Larson brothers.

CHAPTER SIX

The Larson brothers had settled into the farm and tried to maintain the property, so no neighbors or passerby would be aware the old farmer was dead. They sold off the livestock because they had no desire to tend to any animals. They had a full pantry of food and a basement full of booze, so they put the money in a coffee can for down the road. They had no plans to leave the farm, but that could change at any point in time. The two brothers started drinking early that day. At around three in the afternoon, Jeff left to get gas for the car ten miles east of the farm. He returned approximately an hour later. In the trunk of the duster, he had the unconscious body of a young, blonde female. They moved her to the living room couch and continued to party. They did not bother to tie her up; she had no place to run to, and the nearest farm was a four-mile walk. When she came to, the brothers took turns raping her. She screamed and struggled, and James mocked her as he repeated over and over that no one could hear her. When they were done, they threw her to the floor and poured a whole bottle of whiskey over the poor girl's body. They laughed and chanted, "The whore wants more, the whore wants more." Later that night, when they were done, they dragged her to the barn. They strung her up by the neck and gutted her like a pig and laughed and watched her die. They cut her body up with a chainsaw and put the remains in a blue recycling bin. They drove twenty miles west of the farm, and in the shroud of darkness, dumped the remains all over the highway. The next day by the time the police found her, multiple vehicles had repeatedly drove over the body; only the head was intact.

The New York Highway Patrol was the first on the scene. They dispatched the NYPD, and they contacted Coop Porter right away. By the time Case and Coop arrived, an ambulance had bagged the head, and the police had cordoned off the area. Two officers were literally shoveling the remains off the road, and three others were puking on the shoulder of the road behind a cruiser. The road was soaked with blood, and guts and bone fragments large and small were scattered everywhere. Thousands of flies were everywhere, and the heat of the sun only intensified the smell of rotting flesh. Case had no sooner opened the door of the car when he, too, began to puke. Twenty cop cars and three fire trucks and two ambulances blocked the road on both sides to prevent any spectators from viewing the horrendous sight. They scrapped up what remains they could, and the fire trucked hosed down the road to remove the leftover blood. They cleared the highway as quickly as possible, so the traffic that was piling up could get moving and they could open the road. The majority of the cruisers, fire trucks, and ambulances left the scene. Case and Coop stayed behind to briefly converse with the highway patrol officer. Coop only asked the officer two questions. The first was if he was okay, to which he replied yes. The second question was an inquiry about pictures. He told Coop that he had the dash cam on the whole time and that he had also taken multiple shots from his cell phone. Coop instructed him to clear it with his superiors and email him copies of everything ASAP. Coop wrote down his email and cell number, handed it to him, and then they drove away. The two men were in no mood to finish the rest of their shift; they booked it off and drove home. The two friends did not have much to say to each other; all Case kept thinking was that maybe he should pack it in and retire. Enough was enough.

Summer was winding down, and Paul and his father visited New Jersey every chance they got. This long weekend, they were planning something special for Laura. Their neighbors, Janet and Fred, flew in from Chicago. Nancy and a few of her close friends had organized a surprise baby shower for her daughter-in-law. The house was a flurry of activity when the two men arrived late Friday night. Paul was exhausted from the drive but elated to see his family. Nancy had saved dinner for them, and they both ate and joined everyone on the porch for a spirited get together. Paul was content but unusually quiet; he was a man with things on his mind. Fall was coming, and the boys would be going back to school. The new baby would be arriving soon. He wanted his family home. Janet and Fred's home had sat vacant the whole summer; he wondered what their plans were. Now was not the time, but he and his wife had to deal with the situation at some point. The next day, the baby shower finished late in the afternoon, and Laura retired for a short nap before dinner. Janet was tending to the baby, and Nancy was putting some of the food away. As it turned out, Paul, his father, and Fred were the only ones sitting on the front porch. Paul looked directly at his friend and voiced his concerns. Shaking his head, Fred whispered, "Hell if I know Paul I got just as much riding on living in Cold Spring as you do. The hardware store is closed, and my house is sitting in limbo. I am sure you're aware the market value for both our homes is shit. I would love any input you got because the way I see it, I am fucked.

"The other side of the coin is my family is in danger. So, for the second time, I am fucked. I vote we have another drink, my friend, since we are both fucked."

As bleak as things were, they all managed to chuckle over the way Fred kept saying fucked. Fred always believed it was better to laugh than cry, and this occasion was no different. As they poured another scotch, Fred said, "Cheers, and welcome to the fucked club." They all started to roar.

Around 9:00 P.M., Paul's parents turned in for the night, and the two couples decided to take a short stroll. As they walked, the subject about Cold Spring came up again. This time Fred had a totally sober approach about the topic. He told Laura and Paul that if things did not change fast, his business and home were gone. He pointed out that he did not have patients depending on him and that he had other stores and it might be in his best interest to close up shop and move. He pointed out that his home was worthless, but he did not care. His attitude was burn it or give it away, as long as his family was safe. Paul shared his sentiment but was not in the same financial spot to walk away. Laura squeezed her husband's hand. Paul turned to gaze at her and put his hands on her cheeks and kissed her softly. Janet giggled and blurted out, "I swear, sometimes you guys are worse than two horny teenagers."

Paul just kept on kissing his wife and feeling her ass. When he was done, he looked directly at Janet and exclaimed, "You're just jealous. We all know, woman, you want in the good doctor's pants."

They all laughed, and Janet wacked him in the back and said, "In your dreams, buddy, in your dreams."

Fred grabbed his wife and kissed her, too, and rubbed her ass. When he was done, he looked at Laura and teasingly said, "Hardware store owners got nice tools." They all laughed, and Laura told them they were all nuts. They all laughed even harder because of her choice of words. It was a beautiful night, and even though they were enjoying their stroll on the boardwalk, they decided to get home. They all wanted to check on their kids. As they settled in to enjoy a movie and eat some popcorn, Laura thanked them all for the lovely baby shower. She felt sad that their daughter had to come into this world amidst such terrible circumstances, but she did not share her thoughts. Almost as if Paul could read her mind, he reached over and lovingly rubbed her stomach and gently smiled. That night when they went to bed, Paul held her and told her not to worry, he would do everything and anything to protect his family. They made love and fell asleep holding each other.

Paul meant what he said; Laura was due in three weeks, and he had no intention of letting anyone hurt them. He told no one that he had purchased a gun three weeks back. He had been practicing at the gun range two days a week. He stored it in a hidden compartment in his kitchen under the dishwasher, and it was loaded. If the son of a bitch even so much as stepped on his property, he would not hesitate for one second about taking his life. He did not care about the law; sometimes drastic times called for drastic measures. This time around, no one was going to harm his family or friends on his watch. Fall had arrived, and the leaves were beginning to turn bright colors. Paul and his father again made the long drive to New Jersey. He was elated and nervous about the pending birth of his child and could not wait to get home. The baby arrived two days later and was totally healthy and weighed seven pounds, six ounces. They named her Ashley Elizabeth, after his mother. Paul closed his doctor practice for two weeks and stayed and spent some quality time with his family. The following Sunday, they had an early traditional Thanksgiving turkey dinner, with all the trimmings. They felt it was best because all the family was together, and in November, they might not be. His mother made two pies apple and pumpkin for dessert. Fred and Janet flew in again to celebrate and to see the new addition to their family. It was a hot fall day, and everyone was having a great time when Paul's cell phone began to ring. He was surprised to learn it was the sheriff from Cold Spring on the other end. Case informed him that his office had been broken into and completely trashed. He apologized to Paul, telling him he did not mean to ruin his day, that he just thought he should know. Case left out the part about the chopped doll parts in a box covered with pig's blood. Paul did not say a word; nothing was going to spoil the time with his family. As Case hung up the phone, he could not help but wonder what this sick fucker fixation with the good doctor was all about.

The following week, Paul returned to Cold Spring. He made some calls and had a contractor come in and clean up the office and do any needed repairs. It was not as bad as he thought it would be, but he still was not very happy about the whole situation. The same day he paid a visit to the sheriff's office. Case recognized him and immediately shook his hand. Paul asked him if he had an idea who had ransacked his office, and Case told him they had dusted for prints, but the results had not come back yet. Paul was not in the mood to play games and abruptly announced that they both knew full well who it was and, off the record, if the man came anywhere near his property that he had every intention of killing him. He coldly stared at Case and told him, "You better pray you find him first." Case understood how he felt but advised him that taking the law into his own hands was not the solution to the problem. Paul told him to go fuck himself and angrily walked out of the precinct and kicked the door behind him. He got into his car and laid rubber as he left the parking lot. Paul was a very patient man and did not have a short fuse, but this garbage had gone on long enough. By the time he reached home, he had calmed down but was seriously contemplating calling the news media. Why not? The police force sure seemed to be doing sweet fuck all about finding him; maybe the media broadcasting his pictures would get results.

It is hard to be happy when every single day your family has to endure hardship. What makes it worse is that it's tough to find no answers, leaving no hope and being forced to just live with it. He could immerse himself in work, but every second of every day, the danger loomed. He was celebrating the birth of his daughter and suffering from separation anxiety at the same time. No one had any recommendations. He never thought of himself as emotional, but he was tired, angry, defeated, and depressed. These feelings had slowly manifested after the death of Molly Turner. The remorse he felt over his daughter's dead was catastrophic. He found himself experiencing the same agonizing heartbreak. The feelings of inadequacy overpowered it all. He felt he had failed miserably to protect both girls. Laura had never blamed him or held him responsible. They were united in heartache. There were no clues, no leads, nothing. The information died, the story died, and along with it, part of Paul died. In the end, you just learn to live with it, but you never come to terms with it. Late at night, he often wondered if her parents felt the same as him. They were not perfect parents, but who is? Just because you make mistakes does not mean you do not love your kids. He was absolutely sure they felt the same feelings of guilt and remorse. Through it all, the thing that scared him the most was the rage that was growing inside him. There was no doubt in his mind that he was capable of killing. If that meant the sacrifice of his own life, that was okay. So be it.

He wanted revenge. He wanted back what was taken from him and his daughter. His belief of the greater good had been ripped away. His daughter's innocence and life were stolen. When trust, faith, hope, and love are taken, they can be restored, but not innocence. Childhood innocence is the worst thing anyone can ever take from you. It is a reality we all face at some point, and we realize the world truly is not a wonderful place. Children don't view the world the way adults do. They have no distain, disgust, hate, or anger. The negative emotions and beliefs are taught to them by an adult. Only a child would perceive heaven as a beautiful, loving place because that is the reality they exist in. If they still have their innocence intact, that is their perspective. As Paul and his dad sat on the porch after dinner, a cruiser pulled up. Case Porter got out of the car and strolled toward the house. Paul looked at him with the same cold stare. As Case leaned on the railing of the porch steps, he apologized to Paul. He shared pertinent information about the investigation that immediately confirmed Paul's suspicions. He went on to describe the deplorable state the girls' bodies had been found in. He expressed his concern and told Paul they needed to proceed with extreme caution. The last thing he said was, "I never meant to offend you. I just need you to understand this man is not only dangerous, he is sadistic."

Paul shook his head and asked Case if he had any clue where the guy was hiding. Case told him they knew who he was, but not where he was. Case apologized one more time, and then he left. The next morning, Case decided, perhaps, it was time to contact the media to see if they could flush this son of a bitch out. He felt at this point it was the only option the police force had left to move forward. He prayed it would produce a witness that knew where this bastard was. A news van showed up four hours later.

Coop warned Case that calling the news media was not a very good idea. The tabloids sometimes use smear tactics and circumstantial evidence. This can include accusing innocent people of heinous crimes. The media can ruin an innocent person's life, put them in jail, or even kill them. The person's personal and professional credibility can be destroyed. The claims can all be proven to be false, and the person can be exonerated. The real killer can later be identified, but the damage is already done. Even if the charges are dropped, the whole ordeal is a media circus. Some victims demand full apologies or sue the tabloids, but the slate is really never wiped clean. Case understood the risk, but he felt at this point, he had no other recourse. The sketch composite was given to the reporter. Case withheld the name they had because of internal politics and morbid curiosity of what information they would uncover. He told them that the perpetrator was accused of raping and killing several young girls. The horror of the crimes was compounded by the heinous method of disposing of the girls remains. Within days, the face was shown prominently on the front page of national newspapers and local television broadcasts. The picture was under headlines such as, "The Chop and Drop Killer" and "Hack and Stack monster." The whole thing became a media frenzy, and hundreds of reporters and cameramen were situated all over Cold Spring. In a week, the story began to die, and most of the news reporters disappeared. It was at that point that a news broadcast aired, claiming that the Cold Spring carver had been caught and arrested. A thirty-year-old male who was involved in a gas station robbery was being detained for questioning at an undisclosed location. Within days a lot of the residents of the town started to return home, believing the murders were solved and it was safe. No one was aware that the tip was phoned in by one of the board members from the team at Auburn Correctional Facility. He was ordered to kill the story, and that is what he did. A mistake was made; they did not want it leaked. The police had no one in custody; it was nothing more than a cover up.

The investigation was closed, and Coop pulled the one hundred extra police officers off the case and returned to New York. He spent one last evening with his friend, and they celebrated a job well done and said their goodbyes. Case was now limited to his own staff, once again, and gave most of them some well-deserved time off. He was operating on a skeleton staff to monitor the town. Life in Cold Spring returned to its serene, quiet existence, and everyone was unaware the reign of terror was far from over. The Larson brothers had viewed the broadcast about the arrest, and they had no intentions of letting anyone steal their thunder. They were angry, and it was not long before they started to plan how they could prove they were smarter than the police and could not be caught. Coop had warned his friend, but how did Case or the reporter know the arrest was based on false information? They had been tricked. How could anyone suspect it was a high-powered official concealing a secret pilot program and they had released the brothers? No one was prepared for what was about to come; not even Paul, who was about to bring his family home.

CHAPTER SEVEN

It was late Friday morning, and Paul was relaxing on the porch, enjoying his morning coffee. The deciduous trees were beginning their seasonal change. The combination of colors was visually breathtaking. Fall is a time when the duration of daylight becomes noticeably shorter and the temperature cools down considerably; a time of abundance and harvest and a time for pumpkins, apple cider, corn, apple pie, ghosts, feasts, chestnuts, and a harvest moon. The day was nothing short of spectacular, with a cloudless sky and brilliant sun shining through the trees. Paul sat quietly and still, watching a squirrel scamper and forage for seasonal walnuts. It all was quite picturesque, but he felt sad and pensive and was not even sure why. His dad suddenly appeared at the screen door and reminded him they had a long drive ahead of them and should get packed and get going. He did not feel like moving but got up and went in the house anyway. Since they had got a late start, they did not arrive in New Jersey till late in the evening. The sun had already gone to bed, and the stars and moon were out. Laura immediately cued into his mood and asked if he was sick. He explained that he thought he was just tired. He had no clue why he felt despondent the entire day.

Case was having a relatively quiet morning at the precinct when calls started to pour in. He received multiple complaints about missing pets and posters all over town saying, "Catch me if you can." It was more than likely some sick, teenage prank. Sometimes the boys in town got bored and vandalized the local businesses. It ranged from anything from spray paint to damaged property. Sometimes they mooned people, slashed tires, and smashed windows. Bill Pratt was the leader and the worse of the bunch. Case was in no mood to deal with it, so he sent one of his deputies. He headed over to the local mini mart, where the boys were known to hangout. He warned the boys to stop stirring up trouble, or he would charge them with trespassing and put them up in county lockup for the night. An hour later, more calls poured in, and this time, residents were complaining about finding dead animals on their doorsteps. Case instructed his deputy to personally drive the four boys home and get him one of the posters, so he could have it handy when he spoke to the parents. Case went home, not giving the matter another thought. On his way, he stopped off at the liquor store on Main Street, and as he was leaving, he walked by an old, black Plymouth Duster with two, dark-haired men in the front seat and thought nothing of it. In the trunk of the car, James and Jeff had an unconscious ten-year-old girl. Should he have sensed the pending danger? Should he have read the warning signs? Are there times you regret a moment? Times you look back on things and wished you had just done something different?

It's that ripple in time you can't recover or fix, and you regret it the rest of your life. You make an effort to minimize it in your mind, knowing it is not your fault, but it changes nothing. The following morning when the call came into the precinct about the dead body in the park, Case instantly realized the posters and dead animals were no prank. When the officers arrived on the scene, they found a dead girl nailed to a maple tree. She was gutted like a deer with a bloody note pinned to her face saying, "Catch us if you can." Case felt sick to his stomach; not because he had not seen a dead body before. He was trained to keep emotion separate from the job. What had him unglued was her age. He ordered his men to take pictures immediately and get the body down and covered before any children could see it. A few of Case's men asked if he thought this might be a copycat. Case told them to tape off the area and not to speculate or jump to any conclusions about the situation. Despite the men's mental state, they worked with surprising speed. The only sound was the soughing of the wind in the trees. It blew a few, twisted scraps of paper along the road. This was the third, hideously disfigured corpse they'd seen in the few months. They were savage killings. The girl's pretty pink dress was blood-soaked. It had been ripped at least twenty times, and through the narrow slits of the fabric, many injuries could be seen. Few criminals were this cunning, clever, bold, or difficult to catch. This bastard was escalating, and Case was extremely tense. He stood with his hands clenched, studying the corpse in silence. Case considered himself a strong man, but he felt shaky and weak in the knees. His head was throbbing. He was struggling to keep his breakfast down. He felt sorry for her. She suffered a painful, lonely, horrible death. He tried to divert his attention. But he could not. His focus kept lingering on her cold, dark, blank stare. The child's eyes were empty and sickening. There was no light. There was no life. He could not stand it. He could not catch his breath. He took two, quick, deep breaths, and it produced a long, rattling sigh. Did she beg? Did she cry? Did she scream? Was she violated? Raped? Sodomized? It all was unthinkably cruel. He wanted, he needed to deny the reality of the assault. He did not lose control. His guts were wrenching, but he was determined not to show weak emotions in front of his men. He had a surprisingly calm tone as he instructed one of his deputies to close the girl's eyes. As they pulled the tarp over her head, he turned and calmly walked away. As he headed towards his car, he knew he had lost a part of his gentleness forever.

They had no viable leads. Case felt outraged and frustrated. After he returned to his office, he sat brooding. He held his head in his hands, rubbing his brow, pondering the gravity of the situation.

In New York it was 1:00 P.M., and Coop Macy was sitting reading the morning paper. When the phone rang, he picked up the receiver and blurted out, "Coop Macy's office." There was a moment of silence. It was Case Porter. He almost sounded panicked. He stammered as he choked out the words… "I have something you won't believe." Coop listened intently as his friend laid out the sorted details of the girl in the park.

Coop swore, "Fuck me." He instructed Case to calm down and assured him he would be there as soon as possible. Coops set down the phone. For several seconds, he wasn't able to move. He leaned back in his chair and lit a cigarette. He took a deep, satisfying puff. A few minutes later, he stood up, grabbed his jacket off the back of the chair, and left the office. Exactly eight hours later, he arrived in Cold Spring. As Coop stepped out of his sedan, he was caught in a sudden downpour. As he headed for the precinct door, two officers hurried past him. It caused him to momentarily step back. When he reached for the door handle and was about to go up the stairs to the hallway, Case's voice stopped him. "Down here my friend," he bellowed. "What took you so long to get here?" Coop chuckled and told him to go fuck himself. Case lifted a file box, grinned and handed it his mate. Coop stiffened abruptly. Case grinned again. "Too weak?" Coop did not respond or move; he just smiled. Case gestured towards the door, and the two men headed upstairs. They entered Case's office, and Coop was shocked by the number of boxes. He had no clue what Case was looking for. He hoped he had a hidden bottle of scotch. He knew they were in for a long night.

Coop stood just inside the door. Case glanced at him and instructed him to sit down. As he did, he looked around the office at a gingerly pace. On the second shelf of the walnut bookcase, he spotted two glasses. He stared at Case and nonchalantly asked, "So, where are you hiding the bottle?" Case reached over with his left hand and opened the desk draw. He pulled out a half bottle of scotch and gently placed it on the desk. Slightly laughing, he exclaimed, "See, it's in plain sight."

Coop leaned across the desk, and when he spoke, it was a hoarse, low whisper. "What are we looking for?"

"The question, my friend, is what *aren't* we looking for." He explained to Coop that he had decided to review some old cold case files, looking for anything involving rape, hands, and parks. He figured this son of bitch did not just start in Cold Spring. He suggested they cover all of New York state and surrounding area. He was confident there had to be some shred of evidence to help them find him. Coop ran a hand through his hair, which was thick and black, just starting to show flecks of gray at the temples. He shook his head and preceded to pour two drinks for him and Case. They diligently worked through the night. By morning they had thirty case files they thought might be related. They were tired and decided to take a break. They left the office and went across the street to the café for breakfast. That was when Case notice the black SUV and two men in suits.

He and Coop grinned at each other. They might as well have been carrying a red flag. It was not hard to figure out they were FBI. They were idiots. They stood out like a sore thumb. The question was, What the fuck were they doing here? What were they looking for in Cold Spring? What Case and Coop didn't know was that they were sent from authorities at Auburn State Prison to put a lid on the whole situation. They intended to hunt and kill the Larson brothers. There was not going to be any arrest or trial. They had orders to shoot to kill. A grave mistake was made, and the board of the pilot program had every intention of covering it up. If it was leaked, the press would have a field day. High ranking officers would be charged. The program had already been deemed a failure and was being shut down. They just had to tie up loose ends and silence the brothers. The two men approached Case and informed him they were here to assist in the capture and arrest of the man responsible for the killings. Case had many questions. He wanted to know why Jeff Larson was released. Why had the man only served a two-year sentence for armed robbery? He didn't ask or say anything at all. He just smiled and nodded. His years of experience and instincts told him not to trust them. He and Coop ordered coffee and bagels and returned to the office. As they sat down to eat, the two friends agreed to adopt a watch-and-see attitude and keep their mouths shut tight. Case smelled a rat. He figured the dead body in the park was a solid indication they had let him go again or never arrested him at all. Either way, something was not right, and he knew It. It might have been a copycat or a coincidence, but the odds of that were pretty damn slim.

It was early Sunday morning. Paul's wife was already up. He was awoken by the faint sound of his daughter crying. He lingered in bed, pondering why he had such an uneasy feeling about bringing his family home. He had a great degree of anxiety and doubt. Finally deciding he was being ridiculous, he got up and got dressed. He entered the kitchen, grabbed himself a coffee mug from the cupboard, and poured himself a cup of coffee. His wife smiled at him. She knew he observed Sunday as a day of rest, but she asked him about driving home anyway. He shot her a dirty look. He never acted like this; this was out of character for him. "Paul?" Laura asked. "You okay? You look pale."

"No, I don't think so."

"Want to tell me about it?"

He muttered curse words under his breath. He wanted to camouflage his feelings, but he could not. He explained his concerns and distress about bringing his family home. Without even realizing what he was doing, Paul put the first finger of his right hand in his mouth and began to bite down. Laura reached over and took his hand out of his mouth and gently kissed it. She told him she understood the adverse circumstances of the past months had him emotionally strained and assured him it would all be okay. She reminded him that they had caught the killer. She pleaded with him to just let her and the kids come home. She reminded him that Halloween was coming and that the boys had already missed two months of school. He agreed to her request, but he was still uneasy. They planned to leave first thing in the morning. His parents were sad to see them go but content that the matter was solved. They said their teary goodbyes and left bright and early for Cold Spring.

They arrived late. They were totally exhausted. They got the boys to bed and the baby settled in the nursery and went to bed. A week passed, and they resumed their normal routine and even got the boys enrolled back in school. It was dusk, and Paul and Laura were sitting on the front porch, enjoying a glass of wine. It was a warm, wonderful, fall night, and the colored leaves where dancing across the lawn by the soft wind that was blowing. The street was quiet and peaceful. Suddenly the silence was broken by a high-pitched scream. It was Jane Martian from down the block. She was standing on the curb. It took Laura and Paul a few minutes before they realized what she was looking at. It was a dog running down the street, and in the dog's mouth was a human hand. Paul could hardly believe his eyes. He froze. It did not take long before most of the homeowners had emerged from their homes, curious to see what all the commotion was about. Most of them stood staring in disbelief. A few of the men chased the dog, trying to tackle it. The dog darted and zigzagged across the road and lawns to avoid being caught. He was scared and confused and indignant about giving up his prize. Laura sat fixated on the whole ordeal with her mouth hanging open. It was then that Paul leapt out of his chair and dashed down the porch steps and ran across the lawn. He joined the two men who were attempting to corner the dog next to Janet and Fred's car. Fred suddenly appeared out of nowhere and jumped in the air and landed on the dog, pinning it to the ground. Through the joint effort of all four men, they finally pried the hand out of the dog's mouth and let him go. Fred quickly took off his shirt and carefully wrapped the severed hand in it. People started to cheer and yell words of approval. The men chanted and laughed like they had just recovered a football. The whole street was in shock. Ten minutes passed when Fred and Paul finally came back on the porch and called the sheriff.

By the time the sheriff showed up, a crowd of people had formed on Paul's porch. They were all talking and drinking a bottle of scotch from Fred's liquor cabinet. Fred had examined the hand, and the whole street was already aware the hand was male. It was too large to be a female hand. They also saw the gold wedding band on the ring finger, which meant whoever the hand belonged to was married. As Case got out of the cruiser and approached the house, everyone shut up. Fred handed him the shirt. Everyone's eyes were focused on him as he unwrapped the shirt to reveal the contents. He did not say a word. He closed the shirt and turned to walk away. Fred was the first member of the crowd to speak. He said, "Look, you fucking son of a bitch. You are not getting off that easy this time around."

Other neighbors chimed in, each asking their own questions. Where did the hand come from? Who did it belong to? Was it true the killer was caught? Was it starting again? Were they safe? They were angry, and they were not backing down. Fred started yelling for everyone to calm down. Then he looked directly at Case and said, "For the love of God, you got a family, too. Tell us what the hell is going on. The bottom line is, all we want to know is if our families are safe."

Case looked tired. When he finally spoke, his voice was shaken and rattled. He looked at them all, one by one, and just kept repeating "no" over and over. Finally, he declared they had found another body in the park a week ago.

The last thing he said was, "Take your families and leave." Then he turned and walked away. One of the men charged him and punched him in the head, and he fell to the ground. Fred began to yell again, telling everyone to calm the fuck down. Paul left the porch and walked toward Case. He knelt down and grabbed his arm. He and a few other men helped the officer to his feet. They brought him up on the porch and sat him down in one of the chairs. Fred told them he had a family, too, this was not his fault. He instructed everyone to go home.

It was not long before only the four of them were left on the porch. Fred felt sorry for Case. He could only imagine the stress the man must be under. As bad as it was for all of them, it had to be ten times worse for him. They gave Case a shot of whiskey, and just as he was beginning to calm down, Coop showed up. They all sat on the porch for over an hour. Coop informed them he was bound by the letter of the law and could not give them many details of the case. He shared their sentiment that it was a nightmare. He did not share much information, but he did share his feelings. The last thing he shared before they left was that they were using everything at their disposal to catch this sick fuck. The four friends sat on the porch late into the night. They did not discuss their dreadful predicament. They all felt a profound sadness. They all knew by tomorrow that Cold Spring would be a ghost town again. This time most of the residences would probably sell their homes for whatever they could get. Leave and never return. Janet and Fred left bright and early the following morning. Paul and Laura stayed on an extra day to give Paul time to close his practice. He gave his small staff a severance check, packed up everything, and locked his office for the last time. Laura spent the day gathered up only small stuff that would fit in the car. They planned to have a moving truck pick up the rest. The house had an eerie silence. The boys had gone to say goodbye to their friends. She put the baby down for a nap in the nursery and made herself a cup of tea. As she sat at the kitchen table slowly sipping from her cup, her ears were filled with the squabble of birds outside the window and the incessant ticking of the clock in the hall. On a normal day, the old house and the sounds would have brought her comfort, but today it just made her feel creepy. She felt gray and lonely. Minutes seemed like hours. Then suddenly the silence was broken by a loud knock at the front door.

Paul walked down Main Street. The majority of the shops had closed signs in the windows. He found himself standing in front of Fionne's dress shop. He stood peering through the glass at a striking, red dress. A black SUV was at the curb. The street was usually filled with pedestrians; today it was empty. He shuffled his feet as he moved slowly down the sidewalk. John Walker's modest grocery store was the only place open for business. The Walkers were business savvy and recognized opportunities to make money. Regardless of the situation, people had to eat. He shared his passion with his son, Alexander. Their ambitions coaxed customers with everything from savory assortments of cheese to a superb quality of meats and seafoods. They also had a large array of desserts and fine wines to accompany any meal. It was a wonderful shop. Paul was fixated on the heritage collection of bottles in the store display when he noticed a commotion out of the corner of his eye. He stood, turned, and surveyed them. Four people were involved in a heated argument. He could not hear the content of the conversation, but he was close enough to read their body language. Two out of the four people were dressed in black suits. He did not have a clue who they were. The other two were the parents of his oldest son's girlfriend, Sara Woodland. Jane appeared very upset. She wasn't a woman given to fits of nerves, and certainly not hysteria. She was a confident woman who believed things take care of themselves. It was clear to Paul that she was stricken with fear. Paul slowly approached the group and quietly took a position directly behind one of the men in black. The man turned and starred at him blankly. Before Paul had a chance to utter one word, a black SUV appeared out of nowhere. Its tires squealed as it came to an abrupt stop. Another man in black got out of the driver's seat and quickly ran around to the passenger door and swung it open. Everyone watched as Sara Woodland emerged from the vehicle.

Paul breathed in a deep sigh of relief as his son climbed out of the SUV behind Sara. The two teenagers had been at Foster's lookout point. The two kids were hiding because they did not want to move and never see each other again. Who could blame them? Paul felt their pain. It was their home. It was not fair. It was not right. They were on the wrong side of change. The house was gone. His practice was gone. The house would likely sit empty for years. He knew he would have to start at the bottom again. The sun was beginning to set. The light in the sky was a beautiful palette of colour. It was a combination of blue, pink, orange, and grey. It was something to observe. There was a certain irony to the sunset; it felt like it marked more than the end of a day. We often think of sunsets in other ways, too. It can mark the end of a season, a relationship, or even life. There was no easy solution to their problems, but soon the sky would fade to darkness of night. They needed to get home. Paul urged them all to come to his home to talk about how they could work things out. Jane and Seth accepted, and they all headed toward Cedar Street. The street was quiet, and Paul thought it odd the porch light was not on. The front door was wide open, and the screen door was ajar. Sara was the first one to reach the door. She did not enter.

It was apparent by what was visible through the screen that the house was in total disarray. A lamp lay broken, two houseplants were dumped, and the soil was all over the carpet. The chairs and coffee table were tipped over. Glass shards littered the floor from broken pictures and beer bottles. Broken toys and books lay everywhere. Paul was especially distressed about the pool of blood on the kitchen floor, under the table. Paul's heart was pounding. He thought about his wife. His heartbeat grew even more frantic. He mustered what strength he had and stepped over the broken glass and entered the kitchen. He was fueled by a combination of fury and agony. Sara's father quietly instructed the others to leave and return to the police station, and after they departed, he stepped cautiously into the house. Maintaining his silence, he walked slowly toward the kitchen. Paul was kneeling by the dishwasher, doing something. Seth watched as he pulled out an old towel and unfolded it carefully. Seth's eyes widened as he realized the object in the dirty towel was a gun. Paul was holding a semi-automatic pistol called a Beretta Cheetah. He checked the magazine, and the two men headed upstairs.

The master bedroom was at the top of the stairs. Paul turned the knob quietly and entered. Laura was sitting alone in the dark. Her silhouette merged with the shadows. His gaze moved around and around the dark room. The dresser mirror was cracked. The comforter was pulled from the bed. The fitted bottom sheet was popped loose at the corners. The mattress was semi-bare. A trail of blood led to the bathroom. He cocked his head, listening for the slightest sound. Paul's hand that held the revolver shook, and he gripped it tighter. He was shaking with rage. Suddenly the sliding closet door flew open with a bang. Seth backed against the wall and stood there, rigid and wide-eyed.

Paul trembled, and his teeth chattered. He was gripped by fear, but he refused to succumb. He turned to face the intruder. He raised the pistol with his right hand and squeezed the trigger. The first bullet entered the stranger's shoulder, shattering it on impact. The second shot was more precise; it pierced the man's chest. Thrusting him backwards, he slid down the wall, leaving large quantities of blood everywhere. Paul stared at the body slumped in the darkness. Thinking the horror was over, he dropped the gun. It bounced as it hit the carpet, coming to a final resting place a foot from the bed. Suddenly, as Paul turned, he was tackled from behind. He had no idea there was a second man in the room. The man punched Paul in the face. The blow stunned him. It was painful, unexpected. The man hit him again and again, harder than before. Paul felt shock and confusion. He tried to fend off the lunatic, but his fists only connected with empty air. Minutes passed, and Paul gasped and fell to the floor. The man continued to punch Paul, blow after blow. Only the simple truth was that the maniac was not punching him at all. He was stabbing him. Paul's face was spattered with blood. His white doctor's overcoat was now soaked with crimson spots of blood. Paul could hear squad car sirens and the distant sounds of footsteps as he slipped into unconsciousness. As the gun shots rang out and her husband fought for his family and his own life, Laura did not shift, she did not flinch. She did not even move. Her body, which was abused and repeatedly raped, would recover. Eventually. Her mind was a different story. It was so damaged, so shattered, it was gone. She did not hear the sirens. She did not hear the footsteps. She did not hear her daughter's cries. She was gone.

It was 10:00 A.M. and New York General was its normal flurry of activity for a Friday morning. The head nurse, Pam West, stood at the nurse's station, updating patient records. She hated clerical duties. Her pen made meaningless squiggles on the page. She was still writing disinterested on the reports when Doctor Patterson strolled up to the counter. He looked at her and grinned. He was a handsome, hardworking man but shallow as hell. He was a surgeon and ambitious and arrogant. They exchanged a good morning greeting as he grabbed some charts and slowly walked away, down the hall. She watched him intently till he finally disappeared out of view. She found herself pondering what a sexual encounter might be like with the man. She pushed the thought out of her mind, refusing to think about such things. She was married, and she felt guilty that such thoughts were far from appropriate. The nurses that worked on the ward began to congregate around the station, and Pam moved on to start her daily rounds. The floor was reserved for coma patients, and the majority of the patients were never expected to recover. Paul lacked any awareness of his surroundings, even though he had retained his basic life support functions. His mom refused to let the nurses bathe or groom her son, but they came around regularly to monitor his vital signs and administer any injections he might need. It had been over two years since he had lapsed into the coma from extreme blood loss. The hospital told her his condition would likely never improve, but she refused to give up hope. Every day she sat quietly by his bedside. She read to him for hours and talked to him and touched him lovingly, waiting patiently for any kind of response. She did not care what anyone said; he was her only son, and she had no intention of giving up.

Today it was raining. The dark sky gave off the impression it was evening, even though it was still morning. The rain played a tapping game on the window, and the thunder boomed so loudly that it shook the hospital to the ground. Nancy sat in her usual spot, reading quietly to her son. The lucent light by his bed flickered and cast a bright glow over her son's motionless body. As she turned the page, she glanced up at him. Many times, over the past two years, she wished he would wake from the coma. She missed his voice. She missed his smile. His oldest son was now in college. The baby was almost three. They needed him. Laura needed him. It was a great burden raising the baby, but his parents had few choices. Laura was put in a mental institution and spent her days staring out a window. She had not spoken a word since the day it all happened. The doctors had run every test they could think of and had no clue why Paul did not regain consciousness. Nancy had often noticed her son's hand twitch. The doctors told her it was just involuntary muscle contractions, and it meant nothing. She did not believe them. Paul's father said enough was enough; maybe it was time to pull his feeding tube. Nancy wondered if maybe she was just being selfish. Perhaps her husband was right. Fairytales did not always have happy endings. Life was hard. Paul had taken steps to defend his family and had shot his own son. The whole affair was a sad and ugly tragedy. Contrary to popular belief, life was not about happy endings; it was mostly just about endings. The storm raged on. Months turned to years. Years turned to more years. Paul never woke up. One winter day, a decade later, he passed away quietly in his sleep. Even though the Larson brothers were shot to death by the police, it brought little peace to anyone involved. Laura stared blankly out the kitchen window. She wondered when her husband would be home from work. He was late. She figured she should start dinner. The boys were probably hungry. It was getting dark. Where the hell was Paul?